KT-440-861

A SUMMER BEWITCHMENT

Battered crusader knight Magnus and his witch-wife Elfrida are happily married, but each has their own secret turmoil. Elfrida dreads that her difference in rank with Magnus will undermine his love for her, whilst Magnus fears his deep scars mean he will not be able to give Elfrida children. When high-born Lady Astrid appears, demanding their help in finding seven beautiful girls who have been kidnapped by a shadowy piper, Magnus and Elfrida must work together to save them in time — but what will the cost to their marriage be?

Books by Lindsay Townsend
in the Linford Romance Library:

MISTRESS ANGEL
BRIDE FOR A CHAMPION

LINDSAY TOWNSEND

A SUMMER
BEWITCHMENT

Complete and Unabridged

LINFORD
Leicester

First published in Great Britain in 2013

First Linford Edition
published 2019

Copyright © 2013 by Lindsay Townsend
All rights reserved

A catalogue record for this book is available
from the British Library.

ISBN 978–1–4448–4262–3

Published by
F. A. Thorpe (Publishing)
Anstey, Leicestershire

Set by Words & Graphics Ltd.
Anstey, Leicestershire
Printed and bound in Great Britain by
T. J. International Ltd., Padstow, Cornwall

This book is printed on acid-free paper

DEDICATION

To my husband, with all my love

1

'I am the troll king of this land and you owe me a forfeit.'

Elfrida glanced behind the shadowed figure who barred her way. He was alone, but then so was she.

Do I turn and run along the track? Should I flee into the woods or back to the river? He is close, less than the distance of the cast of a spear. Can I make it hard for him to catch me? Yes.

But catch her he would.

Play for time.

'Indeed?' she asked, using one of her husband's favorite expressions, then sharpened her tone. 'Why must I pay anything?'

'You have trespassed in these woods. In my woods.'

The nagging ache in her shoulders and hands vanished in a tingling rush of

1

anticipation. Elfrida dropped her basket of washed, dried clothes onto the dusty pathway, the better to fight. 'King Henry is Lord of England.'

'I am king here.'

A point to him. 'I kept to the path, and then the river.'

'That may be so, but I claim a kiss.'

He had not moved yet, nor shown his face. The summer evening made his shadow huge, bloody. Her heart beating harder as she anticipated their final, delicious encounter, Elfrida asked, 'Are you so bold? My husband is a mighty warrior, the greatest in all Christendom.'

'That is a large claim.' He sounded amused. 'All Christendom? He must be a splendid fellow. The harpers should sing of him.'

Elfrida raised her chin, determined to have her say. 'I am proud of my lord. He is a crusader. He has seen Jerusalem and he has learning. He can whistle any tune. He defends all those weaker than himself.' *Should I say what I next want to say? Tease him as he has teased me? Why not? Are we are not playing?* 'Go back to your woods, Troll King.'

She heard the crack of a pine cone as he shifted. In a haze of motion, the troll king was out of the tree shade and into the bright sunset, dominating the path in front of her. Taller than a spear, broad as a door, he had a face as stark as granite, of weathered, broken stone. Heavily scarred — *many would say grooved* — he had the terrible beauty of a victor, a winner wounded but unbowed.

A ribbon of heat, like hot breath, flickered across her breasts. He was so magnificent, so handsome. She both loved and hated defying him, even in jest. Striving for calm, she said, 'You will come no closer.'

'Or what, little laundress?'

That tease irked her. 'The clothes and bedding do not wash themselves. Not even for you, Troll King.'

He smiled; a daunting unfurling of that scarred, sword-cut face. The churning heat in her belly swept up into her cheeks and down to her loins.

'I am a witch, besides,' she added, though not as coolly as she would have liked. She saw the gleam in his large brown eyes pool into molten bronze.

'You would put a spell on me, elfling?' he challenged.

'Perhaps I already have.' Her tone and mouth were as dry as the summer. *How much farther can we stretch this sweet foolishness?*

He raised thick black eyebrows, while a breeze flicked and flirted with his shoulder-length curls. 'Is that Christian?'

She wanted to cross her arms before herself, to shield her body from his bold stare. At the same time she longed to strip herself naked for him, unlace his tunic and caress him. Unsure how he might react, she armed herself with words instead. 'I am a good witch, Magnus.'

'Indeed.' Again he looked her up and down, glanced at her buckets, basket, and clothes. 'Should you not have an escort, Wife?'

Do I tell him I sent Piers off to help? Are we still playing now or is he truly angry?

Looming over her, he was close enough for her to touch him. *To caress his strong body will be like stroking sun-warmed stone.* Distracted, she shook her head. 'There is the sheep shearing . . . '

'Done.' He tossed a stack of rolled, lanolin-scented fleeces at her feet. 'I did my share and more and, as I have said already, I claim a reward.'

He winked at her and she found herself smiling in return. 'Forfeit and reward, too, Sire? Is that not greedy?'

'Are we in Lent, that I should fast?' He raised his hand, cupping her face with supple fingers. 'But you are too dainty to linger alone, witch or no.'

He traced the curve of her lips with his thumb and, as she trembled, he gathered her firmly into his arms. 'Any man will try to spirit you away.'

5

'Hush!' She made a sign against the evil eye and wood elves, but he shook his head at her caution.

'I have faith in your magic craft, Elfrida. But a passing knave or outlaw? He is quite another matter. He would see you as a tempting piece, my wife, my lovely.'

'I am not helpless,' she protested, but her heart soared at his loving words. His mouth, as crooked and scarred as the rest of his face, stole a kiss from hers.

He smelled of lanolin, salt, and summer green-stuff, and tasted of apples and himself. Elfrida closed her eyes under his tender onslaught, her thighs trembling.

'Troll King?' she murmured, when they broke apart slightly. 'Is that how you wish me to address you in the future, Husband?'

''Sire' will do, or 'Greatest Knight in Christendom.' Those will do very well.' He kissed her again.

'You rob me, Sire,' she murmured, a

breathless space later.

'Of kisses?' He sounded delighted at the idea, the beast, and grinned when she pinched him.

'Even one-handed I can do that better than you.'

He demonstrated, squeezing and lightly slapping her bottom, chuckling as she thrust her hips back against his fondling fingers. A shred of modesty remained as her wits dissolved into a sweet blaze of need. 'Magnus, what if someone comes?'

'Mark knows to keep them back.' Safe in knowing his second in command would let no one disturb them for the rest of the evening, Magnus sat down in the middle of the path and pulled his wife onto his lap. She was pliant in his arms and as eager as himself, kissing his throat and caressing his back while she murmured endearments in her own local dialect. 'Steady, lovely.' He stroked to soothe her, uncaring that such a tender act made his desire more urgent. 'Steady. We shall not be troubled by anyone, I promise.'

Daily he thanked God for her, his Elfrida. They had found each other two seasons back, striving and facing countless dangers together to free three brides from a deadly necromancer. He had watched her push herself to her limits and beyond for others and, even more strange and terrible, had seen *her* protect *him* from spirits and curses.

Snug and close as she was to him now, his fiery witch revealed another side to her nature; passionate and sweetly submissive. She could dispute like a scholar from Bologna, argue any point, but in bed with him, or sitting on his knee now on this dry woodland path, her loving trust in him was absolute.

He kissed her narrow palms, marveling aloud how smooth they were, in spite of her scrubbing clothes in the river all day.

''Tis only a little charm and some ointment I use.' She smiled at him. 'But I regret, Magnus, that not even my strongest magic can persuade a laundress to remain with us.'

He knew that well enough and he knew why. Of all the women in the world, only his Elfrida and a few others could look beyond his mess of ugly sword scars, his missing hand and foot, and not be afraid. Aside from a constant shortage of maids he no longer cared about his looks, but to have his wife pound washing was another matter. 'It is not seemly.'

'Maybe so, Husband, for a lady born and bred, but I am a witch.'

And a peasant lass, her eyes added, though she was wise enough not to say that. He disliked reminders of their difference in class. To him, it no longer mattered, indeed had never mattered. 'You are my wife,' he growled.

'I am, and proud of it. But see, you helped with the sheep shearing today. Washing sheets and stuff is nothing I have not done before. And now you and Mark and the rest are always clad in clean linen and woolens. Do you remember the stinking heap of filthy clothes I discovered at your manor when we first arrived?'

Magnus knew he was losing this. 'Let me pay a laundress in gold.'

She tugged on his chest hairs, a tingling reproof. 'And then our woman cook would be offended, and my own spinning maid. They would demand more, and so would the male head cook and the farrier.'

He kissed her before she named every servant in the place. 'Can you not give me a philter to make me less ugly?' he teased.

'Hush, you.' She wormed a soft hand through his tunic laces and touched his strongly beating heart, flesh against flesh. 'As I have said before, you are most handsome, especially from the back.'

She laughed up at him, her amber eyes bright with mischief.

'Have a care, or I might say the same — and do more.' Cupping her backside again, he savored how her lashes trembled and her face flushed in response to his caress. He spanked her lightly on her nether curves and she wrapped her arms tight about his neck.

'Magnus,' she breathed, snuggling into the crook of his arm, clinging as he drew her scarlet skirt up her legs and tucked it round her slender middle. 'Sir,' she whispered, as he rolled her off his lap and onto her back, taking care her head was pillowed by the sheepskins.

* * *

'We should move,' Elfrida managed to say, some uncounted time later. Languid, almost sinfully relaxed, she lounged on top of her husband, wishing they could stay as they were.

'Not yet,' grunted Magnus, trapping her legs with one of his and hugging her. Matching her mood, he only opened his eyes when she leaned up on him. 'Watch those needle elbows, Wife.'

'I need more of those.'

'Elbows?'

'Needles. Christina wants me to make her some clothes.'

'For her and her coming babe, no doubt.' Magnus yawned and kissed her elbow. 'Your sister and Walter are still visiting for the midsummer?'

Elfrida nodded. 'Just after Saint John's day. Unless you do not wish it?'

He shook his head, showing his crooked smile. 'Christina and her husband are always welcome at our house, elfling.'

Even though she chatters endlessly of babies, as she once used to gossip about her wedding day. Magnus was too gracious a host to admit that. For an instant he did seem about to say more, but then he tipped her off him and rolled swiftly to his feet.

'Get behind me,' he whispered. 'We are no longer alone.'

How did Magnus hear and sense that when I did not? True, he is a warrior and these are his woods, yet I am the witch! Am I so transported and undone by our lovemaking as to be half blind after? Should I be? Is that a fault? Has my marriage diminished my powers of magic?

Faster than quicksilver the questions rushed through her as Magnus stood and straightened, standing before her as a shield. She reached out beyond him with her mind, seeing Mark dashing along the track, the low sun glinting on his ginger hair. She heard his panting breath, caught glimpses of his thoughts and understood his alarm.

She touched Magnus's shoulder. 'Mark comes with news of strangers. Not knights or crusaders, pilgrims or travelers, some others. One is a woman.'

'A laundress?'

'A lady, I think,' Elfrida replied, feeling as nervous as Mark looked. *A lady! How do I greet her? Is the hall swept and clean? Is there enough food, enough fine bread?* 'She and her companion want your help. They will ask you for it soon.'

She tried to smile, but Magnus knew her too well to be fooled by her calm words. Without taking his eyes from the

13

careering Mark, he reached behind himself and took her hand in his.

'*Our* help, Lady Elfrida. Ask for one of us and they will have the pair of us, yes?'

'If the cause is just, for sure, yes.'

As she spoke, a sweet-sour taste filled her mouth, as if she had bitten on a crab apple. Elfrida swallowed the bitterness and checked her skirts, smoothing her clothes and ensuring her mass of red hair was hidden beneath her veil. Wishing she was wearing something better than her faded scarlet, she prepared to hear more.

2

The lady was a golden blonde, Elfrida guessed, glancing at the woman's pale eyebrows and flawless, freckle-free skin. She was taller than many, lissome and shapely, and moved in her dark blue gown as if accustomed to praise and attention. Her light-blue veil matched her eyes and her belt also was blue, tipped at each end by a tinkling fragile silver bell.

Her laugh, when she chose to laugh, was deep and mellow, like her voice. Elfrida envied her that, and the way she gripped every man in the great hall, including her husband.

Magnus is paying attention to a strange tale, as you should be, but must the lady smile so freely? Elfrida was annoyed. The woman had not even blinked when meeting her fierce warrior for the first time, which told Elfrida that the lady had heard of her famous questing knight and his sword-scarred face.

Of course she knows of him. That is why she has come.

And Magnus was listening, still as a stone gargoyle. Mark and the rest of his men stared at the woman sitting on the guest chair on the dais, tracking her every move. She toyed with her cup of ale and dish of strawberries and cream.

Strawberries I picked for her from our garden, and ale I made.

Elfrida frowned, disliking such petty thoughts. Thus far, the lady had not directly addressed her. The lady had been escorted into the hall by two richly-gowned young women and she had pointedly not hidden her surprise at Elfrida's lack of attendants. The lady had introduced herself in French and Elfrida did not know her name. She could not warm to the woman.

'You speak the native tongue?' the lady had remarked in the local dialect of Norton Mayfield when Magnus replied in English. She gave another of her pretty laughs and the silver bells on her belt trembled. 'Now I know I am not in Winchester or London.'

See if London or Winchester can help you with your problem, lady. Smiling behind her cup, Elfrida had drunk deeply to hide her distaste.

Now she hastened to recollect as Magnus turned to her on the bench. 'What do you think, Wife?'

'Wife? I thought her your mistress or leman . . . ' The lady leaned forward on her seat and granted Elfrida a swift, assessing glance, her gaze lingering below the belt of Elfrida's shabby scarlet gown.

To check if I breed yet, which to her is all my kind can do. She must think I captured Magnus by becoming pregnant.

'I introduced Elfrida as my lady,' Magnus continued steadily, his brown eyes gleaming. 'She is deep in my confidence. What thoughts have you, Elfrida, on the Lady Astrid's dilemma?'

Bless him for telling me her name!

Names were important, a name always gave her more. Meeting Astrid's hastily composed face, Elfrida remained calm as a piercing sense of certainty flashed through her, followed by anger.

'You need my lord's help?' she asked the woman directly.

Lady Astrid nodded, but her clenched hands showed her dislike of admitting this.

'His help to trace and recover kidnapped children and infants?' Elfrida persisted.

'Not infants,' corrected Lady Astrid stiffly. 'Six young maids, aged between eleven and fourteen. Six small, pretty, peasant girls.'

'And you believe they have been kidnapped?'

'I know they have been taken from their families and villages by a stranger, an evil stealer away of innocents. I cannot find them. Your husband is a famous hunter and tracker, so I have come to him.'

'So, what do you think, Elfrida?'

18

repeated Magnus.

Mainly that Lady Astrid does not want to ask for aid. She is a noble chatelaine, once married beneath her rank, now widowed. She seeks to recover power, not children.

'Only that this stealer of innocents has charmed or stolen away more than the half-dozen village and country girls whom the lady has mentioned.' Elfrida noted the widow's expression never changed but her youngest maid, hovering behind her chair, stopped breathing for an instant, and the handsome priest seated beside her looked away.

'There is one more missing child, is there not?' Elfrida asked, prompted by intuition. She saw Lady Astrid's slight, unconscious nod of agreement and knew she was right. She now drove home her point. 'The stranger to the lady's lands and villages has also kidnapped a child of great fortune, a special child, whom Lady Astrid must find.' Lady Astrid wiped her mouth and sighed. 'That may be true . . . Elfrida, but if you and your lord find the other lost little ones, then you will also discover her. I told of the many to show the urgency of this matter.'

'No, you heard my lord is kind and generous and you strove to touch him by an appeal to his heart, rather than to his head. You did not want to mention the special one, because a secret is power and you have much to lose here, I think.'

She does not want to admit it. Braced for the woman's dismissal of her, Elfrida saw the icy flash in Lady Astrid's speedwell blue eyes, the tightening of her pink lips. She had just made an enemy. *No matter, there are still the missing innocents, the six young maids, stolen from their families.*

'One or six, a lost child hauls on the heart-strings.' Magnus drained his cup, signaled for another. He glanced at Elfrida, a question stark in his face, and she nodded. 'We shall help you,' he promised.

Elfrida pushed aside her cup and

plate and leaned her elbows on the trestle, careless of the lady's raised brows. 'I may be breaching good manners, but you still need me,' she said bluntly. 'Tell us how the special one came to be taken.'

'Why her alone, Elfrida, if you claim to care for the other girls?' the lady flared, not troubling to be amiable now she had Magnus's promise. The priest muttered a reproof in French. Lady Astrid drummed her fingers on the trestle.

That sign of irritation made Elfrida like Astrid a little more, but she did not soften her reply. 'She is the one you need, the one you and yours paid great attention to. I am sure you cannot swear to how the others were stolen away, but you will know about her. Tell us again, beginning with her name.'

Lady Astrid said nothing. It was the priest who had come with her who answered. 'She is the only daughter of my lady's cousin, who has estates in England and France. Rowena is eleven years old, small for her age, with dark hair and blue eyes. She is a bold child, curious and sanguine.'

'A good lass,' Magnus remarked, 'and in your care, Lady Astrid?'

Poor child, if that were so. Struck by the image of a dark, wide-eyed little girl, trying to be brave because she knew she was not wanted, Elfrida hid her fingers beneath the table lest they tremble.

'In mine also,' the priest answered. 'Rowena is destined for the church. Her father swore her postulancy for her as payment of a tithe.'

'Should the father not have waited to see if Rowena has a vocation?' Magnus was asking what Elfrida wanted to know.

'Is that relevant, my lord?' Lady Astrid countered, favoring Magnus with a sweet smile.

'It could be very important if the girl hated the idea and ran away,' Magnus went on mildly. 'She may be missing to you, but not kidnapped.'

'Or if Rowena went willingly with the child stealer,' Elfrida dropped in.

★ ★ ★

Magnus felt the sudden silence in the hall scrape against the back of his neck and knew his little witch had hit the target. Waiting for the priest to respond, he regretted that Elfrida and Lady Astrid had clashed. His wife missed female company and rather more stimulating companionship than her sister's, but Astrid was an aristocrat. Despite her winning ways, pride and making a show of status was bred into her. Even though haste was needed in this matter of the kidnapped youngsters, he should have thought to warn Elfrida to change her gown, to wear the jewels he had given her, before she rushed into the great hall.

Splendor in Christendom, admit it, man! Astrid irked you with that stare at Elfrida's belly. Foolish as his wife's sister might be, she was already pregnant. The family was fertile, so what did that make him? *Can I give her a child? Are my war wounds affecting that?*

Worse, Elfrida was a wise-woman as well as a witch, so if he should speak to anyone on this delicate matter it should be her, yet pride made it impossible. He knew that he had not been struck in his parts — and by God they worked well for him — but he had been badly injured, so perhaps his seed was damaged.

I will look to my book, he told himself, and instantly felt heartened. The bestiary was full of marvelous things and useful scraps of knowledge. He would look there and take heed of any suggestions of Greek and Arab learning.

Those folk bred lots of youngsters, after all.

The problem was, this talk of children did not help, but he should attend. The priest was speaking more of Rowena and the strange minstrel who had appeared at his church on the evening that Rowena went missing. He did so in flawless English, giving his name without being prodded, which, Magnus conceded, was a mark in his favor.

'I am Father Jerome, priest of Warren Bruer and my lady Astrid.'

A Norman settlement, Magnus reflected, sensing Elfrida's speculation concerning the bearded, unmarked priest. Was this suave, tall man rather more than Lady Astrid's spiritual advisor?

'Five days ago, at sunset, a traveling player came begging at my church door.'

'He is a Jew,' announced Lady Astrid. 'A solitary, ragged creature carrying a pipe and tabor.'

Elfrida shot Magnus a glance. Guessing what she wanted and, like her, knowing that Astrid would answer him more readily, he said, 'You have seen him, too, my lady?'

'He is that kind,' the lady responded, which plainly meant she had not.

'Was he tall, fair, straight-limbed? What color was his motley? What language did he speak? Did he give you his name?' Elfrida asked, leaning forward again.

'He asked for alms, in a doggerel

kind of Latin, alms by the grace of the most holy lady. He did not tell me his name and I never asked for it. The day was waning and I wanted him off my land before he begged for a bed for the night. For the rest, he was as dark and tall as you, Lord Magnus, dressed like you in a plain cloak and a green tunic, no motley, rather most neat and serviceable, though he was leaner and less . . . hacked about.'

Father Jerome addressed only Magnus, but Elfrida would not be ignored. 'Was the stranger without blemish of any kind? No pox scars? And did Rowena open the door to him, Father Jerome?' she prompted.

'She did, though to tell truth, Rowena was not interested in the man. Rowena was sawing through the hawthorn branches we had brought in to decorate the church and she soon returned to that. I sent the fellow off smartly and thought no more of him until I looked for Rowena to bring her to supper and found her gone.

'The man was young, beardless, some

would say handsome,' Father Jerome added. 'He wore a sprig of rosemary on his cloak and a rabbit's or hare's foot pinned to — '

'Father Jerome looked for Rowena most carefully,' Lady Astrid broke in. 'As did I.'

'Around and about, all the hiding places a lass might choose?' Magnus demanded, thinking they had heard enough of the handsome stranger.

The priest nodded. From his shame-faced expression, Magnus guessed he had scoured the church, his home, and the area, seeking the girl. From Lady Astrid's glower he knew she had set her servants looking widely and had been furious when Rowena remained unaccounted for.

'Did the stranger take anything, leave anything?' Elfrida asked.

'Apart from my ward, you mean?' Lady Astrid flared. 'Stole off with her to serve their rituals . . . '

Magnus blocked out the rest of her complaint and listened to the priest.

'I thought not, at first, but then when I was looking for Rowena I found this, pinned to the church door. Other households where daughters went missing of late found the same token fastened to their doors.'

'Valerian,' Elfrida breathed. She did not touch the little withered wreath that Father Jerome had laid on the table but sniffed at it, then sat back.

'Have you something of Rowena's for my lord to take as scent for his hounds?' she asked.

'Any trail will be old by now,' argued Astrid, but Father Jerome snapped his fingers and whispered an order to one of the hovering maids.

'I will come with you,' Elfrida said quickly, as the maid was about to hasten outside the great hall to their baggage. 'I must ready our solar for you, Lady Astrid. We cannot begin a fresh search for Rowena and the other children in darkness.'

'I did not expect you to hunt or track tonight,' came the cool reply from the lady. 'Have you a bath-house here? My ladies and I would bathe, then eat whatever supper we can in this solar.'

She spoke as if she expected the chamber to be a pig-sty and the food swill.

'Of course.' Her stiff back revealing her indignation, Elfrida rose and sped off with the maid.

'Get Mark and Piers to help you with the hot water,' Magnus called after her, amazed at Lady Astrid's visible arrogance and lack of concern. She may not care for her ward, but if she wanted her back the lady was going about matters in a queer way and not gaining allies. *I know Normans are ruthless, but even so.* Dismissing her for the moment, he determined to ask the priest more about Rowena.

Elfrida knows something more, too, and when we are bedded down in the great hall tonight and can talk together, I will know it, or sooner yet.

Yes, sooner yet . . .

★　★　★

Stuffing fresh hay and sleeping herbs into the great bed in the solar, Elfrida considered what she had learned from Father Jerome and the youngest maid, Githa. An elegant, pale young woman sporting many bracelets, Githa had spoken freely of her noble mistress Lady Astrid and the child Rowena.

'She lived with my lady and we visited Father Jerome's house in Warren Bruer every week,' Githa was saying, while Elfrida helped her carry the lady's jewel boxes into the solar. 'A happy girl, always cheerful and kind. Last week, when she heard that the son of a friend of my lady's was sick, Rowena sent the boy her own pet finch.'

Elfrida heard the lie in Githa's breathless voice and wondered who the 'friend' and 'son of a friend' were. 'Did you see this traveling player?' she asked.

Githa shook her head, carefully clutching a jewel case under her arm. 'He is unknown to me.'

That is a strange answer. If Githa had not seen him at all, she would have simply said no. Something is very odd here. Elfrida cast about for something that might spark the maid's particular interest. Marking Githa's careful dress, she remarked, 'His tunic sounds very fine. I am fond of my lord wearing dark green, for it looks well on him.'

Githa was too polite to disagree and she filled up the silence with, 'The color is very rich. I know the dyers of London produce it, and those of York and Bittesby. I can do this by myself, Mistress — '

'We are going to the same chamber. I am happy to help,' Elfrida replied, wondering if her willingness to do so was a further dark mark against her. As needed, Magnus shifted and carried furniture and chests throughout the manor and pitched in with the harvest and shearing, but was it different for ladies? Her husband, bless him, neither knew nor cared.

Elfrida was alone now, Githa having

slipped back to tend her mistress in the great hall. As she eased the final bundle of the lady's bedstraw and hay into the straining mattress, she felt ashamed and worse, humbled.

I am uneasy and I cannot understand why. I am a witch, a mistress of magic. I know Magnus loves me, that he is as proud of me as I am of him. I am not a chatelaine, but this manor is not a castle. Trifles of costume and manners, even maids and laundry and baths, should not matter. Lady Astrid, for all her fine birth, cannot find Rowena and the other missing girls, but I can and I will. Magnus and I have done it before.

Those girls were older, all brides, my sister Christina among them. Last winter we won them back. Pray the Holy Virgin we can do the same for these poor innocents.

Anger coiled like a dragon in her belly. Rowena and six other young maids were missing and all that Lady Astrid seemed concerned with was her own comforts. Yet what of the other families of the other missing girls, those who were not Rowena? Had Lady Astrid and her priest searched for them? Had any of the families searched? So far as she knew, Warren Bruer was not so many leagues away from here. Why had none of those fathers, mothers, brothers, or sisters come to Norton Mayfield to ask Magnus for help? To ask her?

My magic may be changing since my marriage, but I will surely find these girls. I must.

Swiftly, feeling better in action, she made up the bed with fresh linen, swept out the chamber, then sat on her shallow clothes chest. Trying not to look at the larger chest that Piers and Mark had brought in for the Lady Astrid, she counted up what she knew of the missing girls and the stranger, using her fingers and speaking aloud.

'One and six girls lost, seduced away or taken, always at sunset. Every maid no younger than eleven nor older than ten and four. No girl maimed, crippled or marked. Eldest daughters, younger daughters, middle daughters. All trades, rich and poor, from village or remote country. Fair lasses, brown girls, black maids, red-headed youngsters, thin or stocky, curly haired, straight haired. But all small.' *Like me.*

So many. Briefly she quailed, then rallied.

'A tall, dark stranger, a young man without flaw. A man in green. A man Lady Astrid and her maid may know. He speaks Latin and calls to the Holy Mother. He knows the old wisdom and has some magic. How does he steal the girls away? By music and charm. They have no fear of him. But he must have a place. Neat and clean as he is, he must have a dwelling spot, away from people, and a servant or help-mate.'

'Why apart and why a help-mate?' Magnus asked from the doorway.

How does he steal up on me with his wooden foot? However he managed it, she was glad he had come. He smiled and nodded at the bed, his ugly-handsome scarred face a tapestry of

34

light and shade.

'Good enough for a queen,' he observed.

'Or a troll king?'

A moment, sweeter and more luscious than mead, flowed between them, then Elfrida returned to the task. 'He needs privacy and secrecy and help to hide and keep seven girls.'

'You think he keeps them?'

'Oh, yes.'

'Then we shall find his den.' Magnus threw her a shimmering, slippery scrap of yellow cloth. 'Rowena's head-rail. After some urging of Lady Astrid, I also have Rowena's under-shift in my keeping, also.'

The shift would give stronger scent for the hounds, but this scrap revealed more of the child. Tracing the simple daisy-chain embroidery around the tiny, tender crown of the cloth — done by Rowena herself, Elfrida guessed — she fought to remain calm. 'I must work with this tonight, and the wreath he left,' she said.

'I thought you would need to,' Magnus replied, holding the withered wreath aloft in his great hand. 'Do I escort you to our church, as an echo of the other church where she was taken?'

Elfrida shook her head. 'A good thought, Magnus, but tonight I must work sky-clad, within a hazel copse, and alone, for the length of a mass.'

'Alone save for me. No.' As she drew breath to argue, his fist closed round the wreath. 'Your work your magic by yourself, yes. I understand you must seek these sad lasses and their captor by your means and give me a lead to search by mine tomorrow, but the moon will be high and bright tonight. And I know what sky-clad means. You told me.'

'I cannot be distracted,' she warned.

'Never fret, Wife! You shall do your rites and I will not watch. I shall be looking out for peeping toms and other knaves and then I shall squire you back to the great hall. Pray God, we shall catch some sleep there before Lady Astrid calls for her morning rose-water.'

★ ★ ★

Elfrida laughed, as he had intended, and the tension in her face eased, but she still looked solemn. 'Here we are again,' she said.

'Seeking more missing girls,' he agreed. 'Perhaps if there is a third time, it will be babies.'

'Hush!' She made a sign against evil and rose off her clothes chest. 'I must see to the supper first, or I shall be a poor host.' As well as a poor lady, she clearly thought, but did not say.

He caught her to him before she sped off. 'Let Mark and the cook deal with that, and the lady's bath and anything else she requires. She has made it clear she wants a bath and food but no more of our company for this evening, so we should oblige her. Why not collect the things you need? We can walk to the woods now.'

'Father Jerome — '

He kissed the little frown between her eyebrows. 'Mark and my men can entertain him, if need be, and he may speak more freely with them. As for the rest, you will fast before your magic-making, will you not? Well, so can I.' He planned to take food and drink with them for later. 'Besides, do you feel like eating?'

She shook her head.

'Come, then. You can tell me of valerian and hare's feet as we go.' He kissed and released her, half-smiling as she knelt instantly beside her wooden chest. *She is busy, so I shall look to my book before we set out.* 'Meet me by the kitchen?'

Elfrida, nimbly selecting items from the chest, muttered an agreement.

3

Outside in the warm, still evening they walked arm in arm, both carrying panniers, and Elfrida shared what she knew of the stranger with Magnus. He in turn told her what he had learned of Rowena from the priest. It was, she thought, strangely companionable, but she wished they were speaking of less dark, mysterious matters.

'Valerian is a magic plant,' she explained, skirting carefully around a flowering elder bush. 'It has many uses. One is as a lure. To seduce.'

'And the hare's foot?' Magnus nodded to the elder bush as he stalked by, a grudging acknowledgement. 'The rosemary I know from you is a guardian against evil spirits, so is that good?'

'Because he protects himself from demons and the like does not mean he is not evil himself.'

'Well spoken! The stranger's mention of a Holy Mother?'

'The hare protects him from all danger. It is a creature of magic. The mother he reveres may be the Virgin, but he worships her in older ways.'

Magnus raised his black brows in silent inquiry.

'The wreath he leaves in thanks and sacrifice, of valerian and elder blossom, marigold, wild thyme and daisy, is made of flowers pleasing to the older gods. I have seen such posies left at ancient standing stones and statues, at rock carvings of the horned god.'

Her striding companion crossed himself. 'Rowena is very pretty, so Father Jerome tells me.'

Elfrida nodded, unsurprised. 'And docile, too?'

'Indeed. The priest claims they had no notion she might be in any way unhappy at being mewed up in a nunnery.' He scowled, his fingers tightening on his pannier.

'I have heard she is a kind, easy child,

40

but I do not like it, either,' Elfrida admitted. 'Would you be more sanguine if she was ill-favored?'

'Not a bit!' He glowered at her. 'Do not think to test me, elfling, not this evening, at least. Even without your plan to go sky-clad, I like these matters less and less. Do you know what family the Lady Astrid and Rowena are part of? The Gifford clan! Mighty and proud and wealthy.'

'So why do they ask us for help? Why wait five days to ask?'

'Indeed! The ride from Warren Bruer is less than a day, but with haste they could have raced here in hours.'

'So why not come sooner and then we can begin a search? Laggardly, then,' Elfrida observed. 'Contradictory.'

'Snail slow, and I agree, contrary. And for the rest' — Magnus puffed out his cheeks — 'to them I am a middling landowner and you, I am sorry to say, are utterly beneath notice, in their eyes. They should have far stronger allies than us to draw on.'

'Unless they fear those allies.'

'Do they seem frightened to you?'

Elfrida pointed to a vigorous thicket of hazel coppice and considered as they closed on the straight and slender hazel poles. 'The lady is irked, certainly, but I sense no dread from her, only displeasure.'

'At the interruption to her well-ordered life.'

Trailing a hand across the bright green leaves of the nearest hazel, Elfrida felt a raw sadness, a sense of unrequited loss. 'Rowena seems an agreeable child, yet for all that unmissed. Were any of these girls missed?'

'Perhaps the Giffords do not want her found. Perhaps none of the families — ' Magnus stopped and cursed, spitting to the right against ill-luck. 'That is foul!'

Placing a palm over his heart, Elfrida found it beating hard with rage, the indignation that was absent from both Lady Astrid and Father Jerome. 'The moon is rising. I must make ready.'

He swept her against him in a rib-crushing embrace. 'Prepare well. I shall keep watch.'

'I know.' Wishing to offer words of hope and resolution, Elfrida found herself saying, 'We should talk to the maids of your latest guests, the maids and their servants and grooms.'

Magnus's grin blazed in his tanned face. 'Maybe they have brought a laundress with them after all.' He released her and stepped back with a bow, turning to face the way they had come.

Keeping watch, as he promised.

Satisfied, keeping a steady grip on her pannier, she wove through the close-growing hazels into the very heart of the stand.

⋆   ⋆   ⋆

His wife's magic was often secret. Magnus respected it, since only a fool would set out to deliberately anger a witch. Remembering their early, fierce quarrels, he strove to let her be, to work at whatever she must be doing behind that curtain of crisscrossed leaves and branches.

But it was so hard! To let his woman step between the worlds as she did — it was brutal. What spirits and demons might she have to face? All he could do was guard her body and he would do that well, indeed, but to wait, only wait . . .

I feel useless.

She is the warrior of magic.

So? Forbid her. Now Lady Astrid was whispering in his aching head. *Get her with child.*

⋆　⋆　⋆

Using two leafy hazel twigs as divining rods, Elfrida knelt in the small, bluebell-filled knoll in the middle of the hazels. She was naked, her hair loosened, her feet bare. A slither of a breeze touched her belly like a hot tongue. Distracted, thinking of Magnus waiting just beyond the leafy curtain, imagining *his* tongue against her skin, she wished the breeze away.

'Help me.' Praying to the Virgin, to the mother, she held the rods over Rowena's headdress. Her eyes blurred as she stared at the simple hand-stitched daisies on the yellow cloth, willing herself to search.

'Let these rods divine the treasure I seek,' she said aloud, rising to her feet and circling the pinned cloth, moving sunwise and then widdershins. The twigs dipped and trembled in her numbing fingers but did not cross.

'Show me!' she whispered, thinking of a dainty, pretty dark-haired girl. 'I offer blood as payment.'

She had a knife made of flint, an ancient blade, given to her by her mother. Tucking the twigs into her mass of hair, she slashed the sharp stone across her palm, clenching her fist to make the cut bleed fast.

'I offer sweet as payment.' Magnus had brought a flask of mead for them to share and she had begged him for it. Dripping the liquor close to the yellow cloth, she felt a prickling between her shoulders.

No mortal comes, but the wood elves are close.

'I offer a wheat girl as payment.' She tucked the corn dolly, one she had made from her own lands while she was yet a maiden, between the lush grass stems. The tiny golden figure looked to be sleeping in a green bed.

Green and gold, the colors of spring and summer, blended before her eyes, swirling and dancing in a wild spiral. She danced, too, following the spiral, beating the dry grasses with her heels, tossing her hair, lifting her arms.

The tingle at her back feathered down her legs, and out in the wood she now saw the faces of the wood elves. Shining silver discs in the rising moon, they grinned at her from knots of trees, winked at her through the fluttering leaves. Laughing, they mouthed strange words and nodded to the divining rods roughly pinned in her hair.

'Show me!' she said again, this time a

command. The instant she touched the hazel twigs, ripping them free, she almost screamed at the searing pain in her scalp but the images were building.

Young hands, young eyes, young faces, laughing and leaning in toward her. They turned their heads, showing off new headdresses and earrings, and pouted their freshly painted lips. One girl, slim as a reed and wearing chains of daisies round her throat and wrists, wound a streamer of her dark hair around the hazel twigs, crossing and joining them.

Here. Rowena spoke in Elfrida's mind. *We are right here. We are his hoard.*

★   ★   ★

The moon was still rising. Magnus glowered at it, and at the evening star. His plans of sharing a companionable meal with his wife in the wood, of discussing what Elfrida had learned, had changed. He knew very well what a delectable wench she was when she was naked. Why should he wait?

If she has not done yet, she soon will be.

He turned and stamped through the hazel thicket, meeting Elfrida a few paces in, belting her gown and finger-combing her hair. Lust surged up in him like a thousand Arabian fountains . . .

And below that throbbing delight and desire there was a fresh, cool calculation, his new knowledge of the crisp, no-nonsense advice on human coupling contained within the bestiary, his book.

'No need for that, madam.' He bore her to the ground.

*   *   *

Magnus was not possessed but he was not himself. His face was grim, his mouth set, his brown eyes hard. Even the small gold cross in his right eye seemed to glitter. *Dangerous*, her witch-senses sparkled, but was she not dangerous, too? He kissed her and she

48

took his kiss, embracing his crooked, warm lips with greedy fervor.

I have things to tell him, many things, but this moment is ours and we should take it.

'Naughty,' he warned, as she tongued and nipped his ear and throat, her fingers tracing his mouth, gliding over his body. So big he was, so strong and magnificent, so long-limbed, broad-shouldered, deep-chested, lean-thighed.

'I cannot taste enough of you,' she moaned, trembling beneath his answering caress.

His eyes darkened more and her breath stopped. She heard a ripping of cloth as he hauled off his tunic, flinging it into the growing shadows. At the back of her mind she caught the silvery whisper of the wood-elves' approving laughter, then it was Magnus, only Magnus. Pinned as she was, she could not move and her helplessness was strangely arousing. She reached for him but he scooped her over and flung up her skirt.

'Elf, lovely elf,' he whispered against her ear, his scarred, bristly chin rasping deliciously against her cheek.

'Goddess!' she hissed.

Moonlight fell into his eyes, shimmered through her body and she was lost. Dimly, blindly, she snuggled as Magnus finally released her. Curling against his white-hot-iron heated body, she heard him mutter, 'That should do it.'

Do what? she wondered, then asked, 'Are you asleep?'

A long snore answered her. She said, a little louder than before, 'Magnus? We have to talk.'

She felt him start against her and sigh. 'You are right. Pah, my mouth is a furnace! Have we any mead left or did you use it?'

Both sorry and glad they were out of their own world, their snatched time together, Elfrida needed no reminders of the missing girls, or her responsibility to Rowena and the others. She shook the flask attached to her belt. 'There is a little.'

'Good.' Magnus sat up on the woodland floor, shaking crushed bluebells off himself like water off a dripping hound, and reached for his tunic. 'We talk and eat. We need a plan to rescue the girls, all of them.'

'It is not going to be easy,' Elfrida remarked quietly.

'I do not know,' Magnus admitted. 'I fear you are right.' He crossed himself.

Elfrida shivered.

4

'He keeps the girls and keeps them well, according to his own perverted lights. He treasures them.'

Magnus nodded his agreement to Elfrida's statement, marking his wife's bright eyes and high color as she settled on the grass beside him. She looked gentle and happy, very well used.

She seeks a noble quest and so do I, but I also plan another seduction. Yet, why not? 'Tis for our mutual pleasure and unites us body and soul. Making a child is only part of it.

'Magnus?'

To his instant relief, she was offering him food and had not posed a question, so he did not have to ask her to repeat it. Taking the trencher from her, he bit into the cheese and herb-filled manchet roll. Elfrida had brought his favorite cold food, he noted, feeling the back of his neck prickle with shame.

Attend her, man! She deserves it.

He picked up a peeled hard-boiled egg, garnished with snipped chives. 'How did you persuade our baker and cook to produce such dainties? I was not able to sweep up these fine foods in my raid on the kitchen.'

If Elfrida was surprised at his change of subject she did not show it. She dimpled a grin at him. 'I threatened both with a pox,' she replied, and laughed. 'Truth is, Magnus, I asked them and said it was for you.'

'Indeed.' *That is my Elfrida, for sure. Still, she is a witch, a wise-woman, skilled in spells and potions.*

Including a potion to stop herself falling pregnant?

The disturbing idea thrust through him, an alien dark spear of doubt that he instantly rejected. *No! Why should she do such a thing? I cannot, I will not believe it.*

Quickly, mortified by his own horrible thoughts, he asked, 'In this vision, did you see where Rowena and the others are held?'

Any lack to make a child, if lack there is, remains with me.

And now he had the remedy, from his book.

'I saw Rowena as near as you are to me now and she spoke to me,' Elfrida replied, peeling a second boiled egg with her nimble fingers. 'It was her. She had the daisy as her token. I could not tell where they were, but she and all the maids were dressed in new gowns and jewels. They were not tied, nor kept in a magical bondage.' She frowned. 'Not as my Christina was held captive by the necromancer last winter.'

Silently, Magnus watched her slice the egg in two with her eating dagger, neatly burying half in the ground as some kind of offering and holding out the other half to him.

He took it. 'My thanks. That is good to know,' he hazarded, praying they were not dealing with another dark wizard. 'Can you sense if the lasses are close by?'

'I want to say they are, because I heard Rowena so clearly in my head, because she said they were *right here*, but I cannot swear to it. He seeks to seduce them.'

It had to be asked. 'To what end?'

She flushed and would not look at him. 'To be his wives.'

The hastily swallowed egg stuck like a stone in his throat. 'Wives, now, as young as they are? Has the fellow older . . . wives?'

'That is the question, is it not? I had no sense of any older, or more.'

'But you sense he has kidnapped other girls before?'

Elfrida raised her head. 'He feels practiced.'

So what happens to them when these maids grow older?

Washing away the sickly taste in his mouth with a gulp of mead, Magnus speculated on the here and now. 'Could he have a wagon or a boat? His place of hiding need not be a cottage or castle. Is he there with them every hour?'

'Unless he is rich, he cannot be with

them continuously — but then he must have wealth. Riches and a help-mate, as we have said before.'

'The new gowns and gems,' Magnus agreed. 'Another Gifford, perhaps? That might explain why Lady Astrid and her priest have not scoured the land for her ward, or seem less urgent than they should be. It may also be why they ask me to search — because they are convinced I lack the means and skill to find Rowena. They may already suspect or know who has her. They act as they do for form's sake only, or while they send out spies to find out more.'

'Why do that?'

'Rowena or her close family or both will have their supporters within Lady Astrid's camp. It is prudent for the lady to be seen to be doing something.'

It eased his heart to see Elfrida's extravagant scowl on his behalf.

'I do not care for such politics,' she spat. 'Nor how these nobles seek to use you. But does no one care for these girls?'

'We do.'

Elfrida tapped his left foot and leaned toward him across their trenches. He mirrored her, then lurched to one side, pivoting round to grab the hovering black mass behind him.

'Leggo!' bawled the crumpled shadow, flailing ineffectually. Magnus tightened his grip on the lad, brought him to his knees and pulled down his dark hood.

'You did not come with the Lady Astrid.' Elfrida took in the youth in a single glance. 'Will you have some food?'

'How did you hear me?' came the sulky answer.

Magnus gave the boy a shake to make him mind his manners. 'I am an old campaigner.'

'Your black cloak shows up too dark against the twilight,' Elfrida went on. 'When you arrived a moment ago, I saw you and signaled to my lord.'

The youth's peevish expression changed to one of interest. 'The single tap?'

And thank God Almighty he did not come upon us any sooner as we were

57

making the beast with the two backs, or one back in our case. Glad of that, Magnus decided to release him. 'Aye. Now who are you?'

He heard the lad suck in a great breath as moonlight exposed his ravaged face clearly for the first time but the newcomer did not scream.

'I am Magnus, lord of Norton Mayfield,' Magnus went on, steady and calm as if speaking to an unbroken horse. 'My wife is Elfrida.'

Elfrida wrinkled her pretty nose at them both and he sensed the boy relaxing.

Splendor in Christendom, we finally make progress.

★   ★   ★

'My name is Tancred Olafsson.'

Part Norman, part Viking, like her Magnus, Elfrida thought, smiling as the boy thanked her for a carrot and leek pie. Tancred flushed, possibly because of her smile, then steadied himself by addressing her husband.

'Rowena is my kin and we were brought up together. We are not close kin, not a cousin or any kind of consan — con-san — '

'Consanguinity,' Magnus supplied helpfully. He bit into a pie himself and the two chewed companionably, although they looked very different. Tancred was short where Magnus was tall, a sturdy boy where Magnus was muscled and strapping. Fair, smooth-skinned and amiable, Tancred was very much a page in a great house, with the manners and fine clothes to match. His black cloak alone was worth one or two heavy bags of gold. Seated cross-legged beside him in his grass-stained tunic, Magnus appeared like a dark demon with a youthful charge.

'How old are you, Tancred?' she asked.

The lad's apple-blossom skin took on a ruddy shade again. 'Old enough to ride and follow tracks. When Rowena sent me her pet finch I knew I had to act.'

'So you were not sick?' Elfrida asked, and received a stare from the boy.

'I am never sick.'

'Your age, lad,' grunted Magnus.

'Twelve.' Tancred kicked the grass, then stopped when Magnus glanced at his leg.

'So the finch was a pre-arranged signal. Your parents and kin, will they not be missing you?' Elfrida persisted.

Tancred shrugged. 'I can send them word,' he mumbled.

'We shall do that tomorrow,' Magnus said, 'when I send a herald back with you to return you to your people.'

'Not so, my lord!' The boy surged to his feet, indignant as a ruffled cockerel. 'I came to rescue Rowena! She needs me!'

'You know where she is?' Elfrida could scarcely believe their good fortune. Was it going to be this easy?

Tancred thrust out his chest and put his thumbs in his belt, perhaps imitating an older relative. 'I know where she is not and where she never wants to be.'

'The nunnery?' Elfrida prompted.

Tancred blushed afresh and said nothing.

'Are you also Lady Astrid's ward?' Magnus asked.

'No.'

'Have you searched for Rowena?' Magnus went on.

'Yes! Everywhere I can think of, and more.'

Elfrida hesitated then chose to be direct. 'Do you think she ran away?'

'Why send me the finch, then? As you guessed, that was her signal for me to help.'

'And before you could give it, she vanished,' Magnus observed. 'Lady Astrid tells us Rowena was stolen away.'

'By a dark, Jewish stranger.' The boy flung himself back onto the grass. 'I have heard this news.' Magnus raised his eyebrows, and Tancred added quickly, 'my lord.'

'Elfrida and Magnus will do very well for our names,' Elfrida said swiftly. 'What else have you heard of this stranger?'

'That no one but his victims ever see him.'

'So how does Father Jerome know

what he looks like?'

Tancred started at Magnus's low rumble of a question but said at once, 'He must be mistaken, because no one knows. I know people say he is dark and Jewish, but that is what people always say. The rumor is he has some other girls with him. A few peasants for the most part, easily seduced.'

Elfrida counted to ten in the Arabic Magnus had taught her and strove to ignore Tancred's unconscious, snobbish cruelty. 'Does Rowena ride?' she asked.

'She has a bay pony called Apple.'

'Because Apple loves apples?' Elfrida's question was rewarded by a grin from Tancred but Magnus was more interested in the pony's whereabouts.

'Is the beast missing?' he demanded.

'No, my lord — Magnus. I have brought Apple with me, for Rowena when . . . when she is found.'

Elfrida understood Magnus's question. If the pony had gone it might still be that Rowena had either run away or been drawn away, and it would have made the area to be searched that much greater.

She is kidnapped for sure and possibly still close.

But Tancred's other news, what should she make of that? Father Jerome had given a precise description of the stranger but was that a lie? Elfrida tried to remember if she had seen anything of the stranger in her vision, gained any sense of him from the posy he had left. Dispirited, she heard Magnus assure Tancred that he would not be packed off back to his parents tomorrow. He would ride with Magnus and the other men, ride with hounds following the scent of Rowena's tokens and see if they could trace the girl. Meanwhile, tonight, Tancred would sleep with them and Magnus's household in the great hall, his ponies safely stabled.

Does Magnus want to bring Father Jerome and Tancred face to face and see what happens, she wondered without much heart. As the three of them gathered up their things and set off for the hall, Elfrida kept returning to the youth's dismissive words, 'A few peasants . . . easily seduced.'

We have no tokens of theirs and we should have.

She swore then and there to herself that she would not forget the other girls. *I will rescue them, too, as well as Rowena. If need be, in spite of the Lady Astrid and this boy.*

The vow gave her heart, but she remained disconcerted. Magnus would never be so casually dismissive, would he?

5

Mark lost no time in taking Magnus aside in the buttery of the great hall, shooing away the carver and server while Elfrida found Tancred bedding and a mattress.

Magnus explained who the boy was, then asked, 'Where is that priest?' He had been thwarted in seeing Father Jerome's face when Tancred strolled into the hall beside him.

'In there with Lady Astrid and her maids.' The rangy, ginger-headed Mark thumbed at the solar door. 'Both took to the great bed with possets and potions and blankets and bedcaps, not to mention the good ale of your lady. How Elfrida will manage tomorrow with them, I dread to think. I do not envy her.'

'Any more on the lasses or who took them?'

Mark scratched his nose. 'The priest let fall that the stranger was wearing a pair of fine iron prick spurs.'

'Spurs, yet he arrived on foot, begging like a bad traveling player?'

'Father Jerome claimed he had forgotten the spurs before. Me, I think he was too active attending to Lady Astrid's and his own comforts to remember until she glided off to the bath-house. He followed soon after and then we were busy.'

'Nightcaps and the rest,' Magnus supplied.

'They seem very close, that pair,' said Mark, jerking his head to the closed solar door. 'Our Father Jerome and the Lady Astrid. Sleeping together, eating together. What else, eh?'

Because Mark was an old campaigner, Magnus let it pass. 'But at least they do not join the hunt tomorrow.'

'Mother be thanked! Does the boy go with us?'

'Tancred?' Ever mindful of his scars, Magnus glanced from the buttery into the hall. 'Rowena knows him, so yes. She will feel safe with him.'

He clapped Mark on the shoulder and went to join Elfrida.

I have to tell her she stays at home tomorrow and she will not like it. Yet perhaps if she is not bouncing around on the back of a horse she will take my seed more easily. He did not want to consider the darker idea that Elfrida would want to ride with him because she would be less likely to become pregnant.

⋆　⋆　⋆

'Spurs are a detail and very real, not part of a folktale,' Elfrida said. Part of her was relieved that the kidnapper was as described, but his being a horseman possibly widened the area of any search.

'He will have a good horse.' Lying beside her on a thin straw pallet, Magnus was watching the servers rake together the remains of the smoldering summer fire and dowse the torch lights in the great hall. Close to the longest day as it was, Elfrida could see well in the summer night and knew that her husband was disconcerted. She decided to fight at once, while others around them were snoring and settling. Less than an arm's stretch away from her, Tancred was already an unmoving coiled ball.

'You want to leave me behind tomorrow, but you must not.' She shook Magnus's leg. 'I know I am an indifferent rider, but I can help. What if Rowena is injured? What if the others are harmed? Will a boy like Tancred understand or care?'

'His easily seduced peasants, eh? I knew that would hurt you.' Magnus traced a finger down the side of her face, a slow, comforting touch. 'He will learn better.'

His reassuring stroke glided down her spine and the sparkle of his caress made her toes curl. Elfrida fought to keep on her war charge.

'I should be there and so should Lady Astrid.'

That stopped him, as she knew it would. He cupped her face with his hand and narrowed his eyes. 'You, madam, I can understand for arguing to come on a quest, any quest, especially one concerning young, vulnerable creatures, but our Norman harpy?'

This was a new word to her. 'A harpy?'

''Tis in my book, my bestiary.'

'Along with the porcupine.'

He chuckled. She guessed that he, too, was remembering that moment last winter, when he had accused her of wearing more prickles than a porcupine in their earlier, deadly quest against the necromancer, but she knew she had not won him yet. His next words confirmed it.

'Aye, my Elfrida, and I will show you the harpy, but not tomorrow. I am sorry to say that you must remain with Lady Astrid at the hall and be as nice of a host as you can manage. She will slow us down too much, otherwise.'

He kissed her, slowly, deeply, and the

throbbing in her toes swept over her body.

'You do not battle fairly,' she said, when she could catch a breath, 'and neither do I.'

She wanted to caress him intimately, to join with him, but was too proud to try to persuade through any sexual wiles. 'Make it a mark of nobility to the lady that she can ride fast,' she whispered.

He smiled at her and she felt her heart do a tumbler's flip within her chest. Still she contested the point. *For the sake of the young girls, I must. Even if my wifely instincts prompt me to stay at the hall to please him, the witch in me says I must go with Magnus.*

'Lady Astrid will not want to deny it, Magnus. Challenge her to come. If she and the less-than-holy father are involved in high malice and politics we need to keep them close and watch them carefully. You have a knack of seeing truth. So have I. How the lady reacts, what she looks at, or even what she does not consider will show us much. And it is summer, not winter.'

'Enough,' her companion grumbled. 'You snared me at 'high malice' and converted me at 'politics.' The other poor lasses may be this fellow's food, treasure, whatever, but Rowena — Rowena is different. I sense that he took her on orders but holds her when he should not.'

The tingling heat whirling in her loins had become an itch she was desperate for him to scratch, but his last words chilled her.

'You think Rowena is an heiress as well as a postulant?'

'It makes a grim sense, Elfrida. I do not feel Lady Astrid or her priest have been honest with us, do you? If Rowena is heir to rich estates and if her parents and family are dead, do you see what follows? Even if she is destined for the church, if she is missing, then the church cannot control those estates.'

'Does the Lady Astrid?'

'For a time, at least, while the law decides. Especially if the lady has the ear of our king. If the church does not have the girl, they cannot have her lands, either. They would need to prove she is dead to inherit.'

Elfrida shivered. The whole 'kidnapping' could even be with King Henry's acceptance and approval, she realized, sickened at the thought. 'Dead?'

'I think a marriage or betrothal is more likely. The church would protest but the deed would be done.'

'You think Lady Astrid has a marriage or betrothal in mind for Rowena?'

Magnus trailed his hand slowly down her spine and rested his palm on her bottom. 'I think we speak to Tancred tomorrow and find out exactly who Rowena is, and her parents and kin.'

Elfrida swallowed. To tempt Magnus to continue his loving exploration, she skimmed her hands up his thighs. 'But if the man who took Rowena was meant to hand her over and he has not, does that mean Lady Astrid wants our help after all?'

Magnus patted her rump. 'I sense the lady is seeking her everywhere, by every method. We are just one of many.'

'A famous one of many,' Elfrida felt compelled to add. She wondered how she could discuss this sensibly, when what she longed to do was caress her husband, love him.

'Perhaps. I sense a hasty plan, poorly thought out and acted out at speed. I suspect Rowena's parents and close kin died suddenly and Lady Astrid is seeking to take advantage.'

How have they died? Elfrida sent her silent question out into the ether. She waited, but received nothing back from the spirit world. *Sometimes the spirits do not want to tell or share.* 'Perhaps they sickened.'

'Does Rowena even know, poor lass?' Considering, Magnus paused in his brushing of her back and bottom. Elfrida almost protested, but forced herself to make a coherent reply.

'She may have suspected something, hence her signal to Tancred. But if

Tancred knows that Rowena's people are dead, why did he not say?'

'Because he does not trust us fully yet.'

'It seems none of them do.'

'Those are nobles for you,' Magnus agreed. 'But I do not like the bad planning of this whole matter, Elfrida. Bad, hasty planning and carelessness! Look how this pair in our great bed are concerned with their comforts first, when they should be thinking of how best to recover Rowena. Speed and carelessness breed panic and mistakes, fatal ones.'

'Perhaps they cannot decide if they want her found or not. Yet, Magnus, if they did arrange for her abduction, why not use their own men? That is simpler and surer.'

'They do not trust their own men with this.' The instant Magnus spoke, Elfrida knew it was true.

'Then, for all these reasons, we must find Rowena and her captor before Lady Astrid does.' Elfrida scowled.

'Now you have won,' she complained. *My witch instincts are mistaken.*

'How so, elfling?' Magnus resumed his caress.

Elfrida bit hard on the inside of her lip, using pain as a focus against his tender pleasuring. *If Magnus can reason while we are embracing, so can I.* 'We cannot afford for Astrid and the priest to be with you when you do trace Rowena. We need time to plan and consider how to best help her, without their knowledge.'

Magnus did not smile in his victory, which she took as a serious sign. Again, his hand paused. 'I am sorry, Elfrida. I like you with me, and you questing with me. I thought you had argued your way onto my horse tomorrow, but now I discover you and I have argued you off it again.'

He sounded so downcast she hugged him. 'No matter. You can tell me everything tomorrow evening. You will . . . ' She stopped herself suggesting that if any of Lady Astrid's men rode with

Magnus tomorrow, they should also be watched. If Rowena was found, such men might need to be kept apart from their lady while Rowena's safety and best interest was determined. *Magnus knows this already. He will know what to do.*

'I shall strive to learn more from the Lady Astrid here at the house,' she finished firmly instead.

'If any can, my heart, it will be you.'

'Even so, I wish — Magnusss . . . ' Her breath hissed out as his fingers now skimmed over her breasts. She forgot the rest of what she was saying.

He turned her to her side. Desire, banked and waiting inside her, stoked into sudden, urgent longing. Clumsy in her explosive need, she tugged savagely at his braies, keen to stroke and touch him in return, to whisper love words and praise.

'What?' She was startled when he pitched her gently onto her belly, pressing her to the rushes, tonguing her ear and kissing her mouth. For the second time that night, being pinned by him in such a loving, masterful way spurred her response . . .

The blissful, transported peace after was as awesome as the pleasure had been.

What next? Elfrida thought, drifting into sleep. *Do I care? How very masterful Magnus is these days, as if I am no witch at all . . . Does that matter? What will happen tomorrow and tomorrow night? What . . . ?*

6

Elfrida felt sinfully languid the following dawn, the more so when Magnus took his leave of her with a long kiss and a whispered promise. 'Until tonight, Wife.' He and half his men clattered openly from the manor, Tancred yawning and tousle-headed in their midst, too sleepy to complain at the lack of breakfast.

Father Jerome and three more of Lady Astrid's party had also joined the gathering of horses, dogs and men in the yard and set out. Elfrida watched them leave. The priest's sudden appearance had been a surprise, especially as he proved to ride as swiftly as the others. Waving them off, Elfrida peered through the standing clouds of dust and considered the day ahead.

What Father Jerome and his men do not know is that Magnus has already sent Mark and his best tracker on ahead to Warren Bruer, with half of Rowena's shift for their hounds. They will start at the church there and look for the track of a single horse, tethered somewhere close to the church. Let them find something.

'Please, Holy Mother, let Magnus recover Rowena and the others, safe and well, untouched and untroubled. And let no malice touch his company this day.'

The stranger prays to the mother, too, and he is handsome. But my Magnus is more of a man. The Holy Mother will surely like him the better of the two.

Alarmed, Elfrida repeated her prayer seven times for luck, sent up a wish for calm, good weather and returned indoors.

★ ★ ★

Lady Astrid, on the outside bench, crossed one leg over the other and leaned back. She squinted into the new day as if the rising sun had personally offended her. 'You do not have a stills room?'

'Not yet, I fear,' said Elfrida, keen to talk of the missing girls. 'Tell me, my lady, does Rowena help you with your potions?'

'She had no skill in it.'

'I find such things often run in families. Is Rowena's mother interested in cordials?'

'Rowena's mother preferred to play with her dogs, and to ride to hounds.'

'My lord uses many kinds of dogs in his hunting and tracking, particularly the tracking. When the families of the other girls came to you for help, did they give you anything to take scent from for your dogs?'

'They did not.'

I am not sure I believe her, but she does not deny the families came to Warren Bruer. This stranger, whoever he is, knows that area.

Leaning back farther, Lady Astrid

showed off the lush curves of her body. 'The hunting is reasonable in this country, especially in the royal forest. You cannot ride well enough to hunt, can you? Why is that? Did you learn late?'

'I had never ridden a horse at all before last winter.' *She speaks of Rowena's mother and Rowena herself as though both are long past, dead and buried.* 'And Rowena's father, my lady?'

'A lord and knight, like yours.'

'What is his name and title?' Nobles were usually keen to discuss genealogy.

'William the Fair, of Normandy. But your potions . . . they are really quite good. So how do you manage?'

Sitting beside her mistress, her green-blue gown covered by an apron, Githa was picking over fresh salad leaves. She tossed Elfrida a look of pity.

'By doing my best.' Elfrida continued to stroll before the house, spinning as she walked. She could have told the lady that her whole cottage at Top Yarr was a stills room, the place where she made her more complex potions and completed her most potent magic.

The house Magnus and I need to return to soon, so I may care for the villagers there.

Once we have recovered the lost girls . . .

Magnus was always glad to go back with her. He would hunt and plough and fish with the menfolk, and they would joke and carouse with him. Even the women of Top Yarr no longer flinched or crossed themselves when they encountered her scarred, hulking husband. He was accepted.

He has an ease with them that I cannot have with this lady.

About an hour had passed since Magnus had galloped away and already the day dragged. Crisp in her fresh red gown and white veil, both hurriedly snatched from her tiny chest in the solar that morning while Lady Astrid was still abed, Elfrida knew that she looked more the part of an elegant lady, but she could not feel it.

'Have you any tapestry I can sew?' Hiding a yawn behind her hand, Lady Astrid crossed her legs, one over the other, the opposing way round. 'You Saxons are said to have great skill with embroidery.'

Not this Saxon.

'No? Shall we play chess here on the bench? Githa can bring us my set.'

Chess was the new eastern game that Magnus was still teaching her. 'I cannot warm to it,' Elfrida admitted candidly. 'There is only one woman on the board.'

'The queen, yes. A queen with power.'

'To destroy.'

Lady Astrid narrowed her eyes. 'Can you be so . . . innocent? To understand chess is to appreciate tactics.'

'Magnus is the warrior.' *I am the healer.*

Her fingers tightened on the spindle and the thread strained as Elfrida heard her own grudging responses. The lady was clearly reluctant to speak of Rowena or of the child's kindred, which she found strange and disturbing. Yet as a matter of simple courtesy she herself should be trying harder to discover a topic of conversation that her guest would enjoy, and giving fuller answers. 'Forgive me, Lady Astrid. That was not so well put.'

'*Mon Dieu!* For sure it was not! What if this handsome manor were attacked while your warrior is gone? Have you any idea how to fight a siege? How to preserve this household for your lord?'

The lady's earnestness transformed her from a shapely, blond beauty clothed in black and yellow into a creature of airy fire. Decisive as any queen, she flung aside her own small harp and launched herself off the bench. Sweeping into the great hall at a speed that had her be-ribboned plaits bouncing against her knees, Lady Astrid rushed back moments later in a jangle of silver bells. Today she wore no head covering and her hair was eye-achingly bright, her face a challenge.

Elfrida could not miss the staff the woman carried. *What now? Does she want to beat me, outside my own house, in front of my own people? Why? To humiliate me? Is this how noble women-folk behave?*

Knights, she knew, were bred to fight, but it appeared their ladies were equally belligerent.

'Here.' Lady Astrid threw her the staff, smiling as Elfrida caught it while almost dropping the wool off her spindle and the whole skein of thread into the dust. 'Let us start with simple things first. Do you know how to attack? To defend? Come at me.'

One of Lady Astrid's men, crouched close to the bench playing a solitary game of dice, looked up and smirked. *He expects me to lose or draw back and be whispered a coward.*

Another of the lady's men, a squire with one half of his head shaved, perhaps because of previous illness or worms, called out a warning and encouragement in Norman French.

Lady Astrid has maneuvered this so whatever I do I will be in the wrong. If I am defeated, her party will consider me and possibly even Magnus as weaklings and her pride will know no bounds. If I best her, I will fail in my duty as host.

Enough. I have not brawled hand-to-hand since I was Rowena's age. Tempted to smash the staff into her adversary's ribs, Elfrida touched her own body with her arm. She could do no more because her hands were full.

I do not need any lessons in chess or tactics.

Paling, Lady Astrid gasped and clutched at her waist. 'Stitch. I have a dreadful stitch in my side,' she hissed in French.

Nodding to the lady's maids to tend her, Elfrida guessed what Astrid had said. She felt the same discomfort as a perfect mirror within her body. There was a justice in enduring the twisting pain, she decided, because she had willed it onto Astrid. Calmer now, she mastered the stitch in her side by imagining the bloody wounds that Magnus had endured and the courage he had so lavishly spent, fighting for his comrades.

'Mint tisane will ease you, my lady,' she reassured Astrid. 'Sit with Githa in the sunshine. I shall make it for all of us.'

Praying her face was expressionless, Elfrida walked inside.

Let Magnus be having a better morning. Please.

⋆　⋆　⋆

Magnus knew of many ways to persuade a knight to talk. He could show disbelief or mild interest, so the fellow would brag. He could drink with him, share food with him, spin a tale so the knight would feel compelled to cap or crown it. Bribery remained effective with some, respect inspired a few more to speak out. Straight fear worked on all of them.

In his experience, however, the one with the most to say about everything was the disgruntled, overlooked older man.

Searching on foot by then, Magnus had a balding, red-faced older man toiling beside him as they prodded the bushes and grasses near to the church and priest's house at Warren Bruer. So far, Mark, arriving earlier with hounds, had found nothing, and his own dogs had discovered no worthwhile scent trail. Disappointingly, neither had his trackers located fresh signs of Rowena or her abductor.

Guy, the older knight beside him, had a reason for that.

'We have tried all this already for Master 'I am Going to Pray in the Church,' and found nothing. This wastes time.'

'Did Father Jerome search with you, then?' Magnus asked, peering through the cobwebbed leaves of a holly tree to its dry, cracked-earth center.

Guy shook his shiny, peeling head. He was as lean as a hunter's whip but his jaws were flabby and he had a turned-down mouth. 'He searched the church and his house and yelled at me when my lady's ward did not come running to him. I told him that the other maids had been looked for in their homes and not found; that the search wasted time.'

'What did he say to that?'

Guy scowled, jabbing a branch into a mass of brambles. 'He disliked it but he knew I was right.'

'When were the other maids taken? How long ago?'

'Seven, ten days, maybe, before my lady's ward was seized. The serfs made a great stir of it, and threatened to stop working. Father Jerome promised to bring help to find the girls. When days passed and no help came, the serfs laid down their harvest tools . . . '

So the other girls were missed. Magnus was glad of that.

'My lady herself had to go to the harvest fields and promise the serfs that she would engage a mighty tracker to recover their daughters and sisters. By then the Lady Rowena had vanished, so my lady was believed and they cheered her.'

'And now?'

'You are come. Your men search wells, woods, fields, old houses, ditches and more. The serfs see this and work.' A sly look slithered across Guy's face. 'My lady's men are busy, too, sending and receiving messages and riding out. I do not think they troubled about the other maids, but they strive for my lady's ward.'

So much for my searching skills, then. As I suspected, Lady Astrid has her own men seeking and her own plots in hand. She sought me out merely to placate her serfs. I am here to ensure this year's harvest, nothing more useful than that. Better yet, if I do not find the other girls, the lady can blame me and her serfs will go on working.

'What of Lady Rowena's father? Where is he?'

The shorter man scratched his head and flecks of skin fell onto his narrow shoulders. 'Dead? Five days ago, the same day that Lady Rowena vanished, I heard a tale that Lord William, his wife and his three sons had perished in a great fire, far away in Winchester. Although I have also heard it said that they died somewhere here in the north, of the small pox.'

'But dead?' Magnus could scarcely believe it.

'I do not see William the Fair in this company. Nor his overlord, Lord Percival.'

The Percivals. Splendor in Christendom, the Giffords and the Percivals, two of the most powerful families in England! No wonder Lady Astrid is hedging her bets, delaying all she can, but she plays a dangerous game and now Elfrida and I are part of it.

Has the Lady Astrid any unmarried brothers on the lookout for heiress brides-to-be? Magnus was about to ask the question, but at that moment, rushing through the copse on his pony, dragging both Rowena's pony, Apple, by its reins and a hound on a leash, Tancred burst through a stand of flowering elder.

'My lord!' he yelled, as Magnus grabbed his pony's reins. 'My lor — Magnus!

Mark has found one of the missing girls!'

'Alive and unharmed?'

'Yes, yes.'

This was stupendous news, if true. Glad for the child, for her family, for Elfrida, Magnus bellowed a roar of triumph, but Tancred was interested in one thing only.

'Do you not understand yet? This girl will know where Rowena is!'

'So have you told Father Jerome? He may know the girl.' *And she will speak more readily to him than me.*

Tancred stared at him as if he had spoken in ancient Greek. 'Do you not remember, man . . . I mean, Magnus?' He checked himself, before he said anything more scornful after *man*. 'Father Jerome went off before noon to do death rites.'

In his furious searching, Magnus had forgotten that the priest had been summoned to give faith and consolation at a terrible end — the village plowman had broken his back. And now Tancred was at him again, shaking his arm.

'Come on, Magnus, you must order the girl to talk. She must tell us where Rowena is!'

7

That afternoon, while Lady Astrid dined in the great hall, Elfrida sought out the squire Baldwin. He had been with her and Magnus the previous winter, during their dangerous search for her sister Christina and the other missing brides. He knew she had magic.

A tall, slim young man who enjoyed his food, Baldwin listened closely to her request. Too courtly to pull a face, he nonetheless made his feelings clear.

'To ride with you now to Warren Bruer? Why, my lady?' He did not say them, but the words *our lord will not like it* also hovered on his lips.

'It is necessary. I sense my lord has need of me.' She did not want to say more or admit to the storm cloud that seemed to have coiled itself in the middle of her chest.

This is not my seething disappointment. It is Magnus's, poor love.

'Our lord needs me, Pie,' she repeated, giving Baldwin the nickname she had made for him the previous winter.

'What of your guest?'

'Piers can attend her. Or if she wishes, Lady Astrid can ride on with Piers and join us. But we should leave now. The steward can give our excuses.'

Baldwin studied her a moment longer, drawing his brows together, then smiled, revealing the chipped tooth Elfrida found endearing.

'Do I try to protect you from my lord, or do you protect me from him, my lady?'

Relief flooded through Elfrida. 'We ride and see.'

And pray we reach the place before whatever is troubling Magnus bursts like a pricked boil.

★ ★ ★

Bundled in his cloak, with his saddle cloth as pallet and pillow, the girl slept, curled over like a fern frond. Magnus was glad to see her at peace but felt sick at heart. She had screamed herself hoarse when first spotting him, shrieked herself into utter helpless weariness before fleeing into sleep.

She was a redhead, too, which scraped his sense of shame even more rawly. He wanted to blame Tancred for cantering on ahead and hauling the girl to her feet to face him before any had troubled to tell her that he was maimed. He longed to rage at Mark, who had discovered her cowering in a thicket and done such a poor job of soothing her.

Most of all he wanted to be veiled like an eastern woman. Then he would not have inflicted his ruined, bestial looks on this terrified, confused lass.

Is she even one of the kidnapped girls? Tancred seems convinced of it, but we have no proof. We do not even have her name. How did she come here? Where did she escape from?

Questioning his second in command, he learned that Mark had come upon the girl without any warning, when the dogs had discovered her in the thicket and barked. The child would not or could not say how she had got there.

Magnus did what he could. He ordered Mark to set the hounds tracking again, using the girl's scent. Tancred he sent off with another two of his men to the hamlets and villages, taking a lock of the girl's red hair. He had made Tancred repeat to him what the girl looked like — small, slim, about fourteen, freckles, red hair, blue eyes — until he was certain the lad would remember.

Bad enough for the parents of these missing girls to have their hopes raised by a poor description. His men also knew what the lass looked like, and they would be tactful in speaking to the people.

Perhaps I should have kept Tancred with me, but he would keep jabbing the girl, wanting her to wake. The boy was anxious for his young kinswoman, well enough, but he seemed to think this harried, unconscious girl had no right to any finer feelings. 'She is a peasant,' he answered, thrusting out his lower lip, when Magnus had warned him to go gently.

Was I ever such a thickheaded one as Tancred?

Giving orders, searching where the girl had first been found, those tasks he was glad to do. Returning to the stony roadway that skirted the little wood, Magnus spotted a new cartwheel groove in a seam of mud, but the cart or carriage had long vanished. Had she escaped from the cart? He could not tell.

Rising awkwardly from his crouch, Magnus turned on the road to check on his reluctant sleeper. The man guarding her nodded to him as she dozed still beneath the spreading branches of an oak tree. As he watched her, the flashing gilts of her hair pierced him.

His heart ached and his missing foot hurt as he tried to recall what he should do next.

I am lost.

The worst of it was that he wanted Elfrida here. His caring, fighting warrior of magic was so much better than him at consoling the shy and suffering. He imagined her running along the road to meet him. Both would be united, striving, understanding each other, giving aid to one another.

He heard a drumming of hooves and guessed it was one of his men from the lack of shouts or challenges. Farther along the rutted road, into a faint shimmer of heat, pounded a gray horse with lanky Baldwin as rider.

'To me!' Magnus shouted, before he realized that his squire was galloping toward him anyway — and not just Baldwin.

Peeping from behind Baldwin's back, her face clenched in concentration as she gripped the squire's middle and clung on, was his Elfrida. Impossibly, she had known he needed her. She had known and come. *She comes for me.* Shame of his earlier fears concerning his wife, riding, and pregnancy scorched through him.

Magnus started, then began to run toward her. With every sprinting, skidding step, his heart expanded. She waved at him, her veil flapping like a sail, her long hair gleaming like flames, her mouth busy with an inevitable apology.

She smiles her love at me even as she calls sorry. She thinks I may be angry, the foolish, brave little wretch.

He caught her as Baldwin reined in and before she tumbled from the horse.

I am so very glad she is here but why has she come? What news is she bringing?

8

Magnus was kissing her, murmuring in the old speech. Safe in his arms, making him safe and beloved in hers, Elfrida sank into his embrace. She knew without his saying that he had been rejected, shrieked at again, and only for his surface appearance, the least thing of him. The girl had not heard the sympathy in his voice, nor seen the kindness in his eyes. She had not noticed when he wrapped her in his cloak. She had judged him on his scars.

'Glad you came, sweeting.'

'I gathered that.' She drew back to look at him, so he could see her admiring.

'Baldwin has melted away very quickly.'

'I told him to.'

'And how did you persuade him to ride you over? No, I do not think I want to know that. But how you ride! You must have tumbled off close to a dozen times.'

'I did not want to ride in front of him as I do with you.' She saw his eyes glow at that. 'Who is the sleeper?'

A dart of sorrow, so fast that any who did not know him as she did would have missed it, crossed his handsome-ugly face. 'Ah, now that is the puzzle.'

The girl screamed at him when she saw him and was too horrified to answer questions. Poor Magnus. How vile it is for him.

Still with her locked in his embrace he turned on the road. 'Now you are here, do you remember that charm you laid on the necromancer's servant last winter? The one you said soothed and comforted?'

To comfort him, Elfrida stroked a hand down his back. 'That may not be needed.' The girl could not help her terror any more than her husband could help his looks. *But I can help them both, and I will.*

Having Elfrida by him was more than balm. He was fully alive again, feeling as young as Tancred and bursting with hope. His clever witch-wife understood his need for contact, too. Taking his huge paw in her delicate hand, she led him to the slumbering maid. Then, being Elfrida, she did an unexpected thing.

She knelt by the girl and leaned close but did not touch her. She sniffed the lass's breath, her hair, and sat back on her heels.

'This child has been drugged, very lightly, with a sleeping draught.'

Slowly, she drew apart his cloak and placed the tips of her fingers on the sleeping girl's palm. 'Cool but not cold. Skin softened lately by unguents.'

She glanced down the length of the tiny body. 'Bare feet. Clean, bare feet. She rode here, or came in a cart or carriage.'

Magnus thought of the fresh cart

track and nodded. 'How did she escape?'

'Or was she let go? Or is she another altogether? Let us — '

She stopped, turning her head on one side. 'The Lady Astrid comes. You will hear and see her soon. Can you keep her back for a moment? It need not be for long.'

Magnus snapped his fingers at the hovering guard and sent him off to gather others and delay the coming Norman storm.

Elfrida sat by the head of the sleeping girl. Blushing a little, she patted the grass beside her.

Still shy of commanding me, sweet, after six months of marriage? No matter, you will not be shy tonight. Grinning at the thought, Magnus crouched beside her. His wife shifted slightly so he could see her, the girl, and the road.

'Where are the lady's people, the ones who rode out with you this morning?' she asked in a low voice. 'Where is Father Jerome?'

'The priest is ministering to a dying villager, a plowman who broke his back and who cannot be saved.' Anticipating her sympathy, he added quickly, 'The man lingers but he has no pain.'

He watched her close her eyes and say a brief prayer. 'As you say,' she remarked, opening her eyes. 'He will go in peace, with the sunset.'

How does she know this? She is a witch and knows many things, some I wish she did not know. Magnus crossed himself and returned to more earthly, political matters. 'As for the others, I sent them on with Tancred to the hamlets.'

'They did not try to wake this child?'

'After she had screamed down half the woodland on seeing me? No. Ill luck like that is catching. I know men. We did not know the girl's name and they were eager to leave, believe me, to discover some knowledge they hope will be useful, something they can tell their lady.'

Elfrida looked at him, a piercing glance as if she could read his thoughts, both good and ill. He wanted to kiss each freckle on her forehead, kiss her flower-petal lips and her gleaming amber eyes. The sunlight burnished her red hair and dazzled him.

'You are lucky, Magnus.'

'Because I found you, I know.'

'You are fortunate because the Holy Virgin loves you and for the rest we found each other. Now let me work.' Clearly seeking to take any sting from her words, Elfrida leaned into him. He kissed her lightly, feeling her smile, and then she drew back. He became aware of birdsong again and, in the distance, unseen as yet, the rumble of approaching horses.

Taking a deep breath, Elfrida touched the sleeping girl's forehead. At once her own face lost its habitual animation and color. Bleached as parchment, she closed her eyes.

'Do not be afraid.' Her voice was slower, a little more resonant, carrying a faint echo. 'Do not be afraid, Magnus.'

She is between the worlds again,

tracking the girl through dreamland and sleep. His whole body tightened with alarm, with frustration at being unable to go with her, to fight for her. He forced himself to speak steadily. 'Only of losing you, my heart.'

She clasped his hand, her long fingers smooth and strong as a shield. Pictures sprang before his eyes, a race of images faster than the galloping hooves of the closing horses.

'Her name is Ruth of Lowton. It is her real name. She worked with her widowed mother as a nail maker, a spinner, a gleaner . . . many tasks, sunrise to sunset and into dark.'

Elfrida paused, then spoke again. 'Ruth liked living with Silvester. She met him outside the church of Lowton where he played the pipes. Silvester asked her to go away with him. She said yes because he was handsome and she was weary of quarrelling with her mother, tired of the endless work.'

Handsome. It is always the pretty ones who can cheat and steal and lure because they look good. Magnus clenched his teeth and his fist.

'Silvester gave her beautiful new clothes. He gave her other sisters. She had enough food to eat, and sweets, treats of oranges candied with sugar cone. He taught her to play the harp. When she cried, he cuddled her. He took her with him on the wagon. She was his trusted girl, his good girl.'

Magnus glanced at Ruth. The girl was as still as a sun-basking butterfly through this tale of abduction and seduction, her breathing as delicate as mist. Elfrida's fingers tightened round his and she continued to speak in the same low monotone.

'Ruth broke her vows. She left Silvester because he liked Rowena more, because Rowena, who was a new sister, was younger and very pretty. She left because she missed her mother. She left because she was not going to be first. She left. Silvester thought she was sleeping in the wagon.'

The pretty, the handsome win out

again. But I am glad she escaped. Magnus slapped his fist lightly against the stump of his missing hand.

Ruth snored gently. Elfrida's cheeks glistened with tears.

'He did not care enough to stop, to go back and look for her. *I want my mamma.*'

Magnus's spine and scalp crawled. His wife's voice had become that of a child's, young and lost.

'You are safe,' he whispered, squeezing Elfrida's hand. 'You are both safe. Come back now.'

'*Will you take me to my mamma?*'

'I will.'

At once, Elfrida opened her eyes, gathered Ruth into her arms and sat with her on Magnus's legs. Astonished at her speed and effortless strength, he stared.

'Hold us both,' she instructed. 'Do not let us fall.'

Wondering at the word 'fall,' Magnus wound his arms about the pair of them. 'Elfrida?'

'I am here with you.' Elfrida tucked Magnus's cloak about the girl and eased her arm beneath Ruth's head. She watched Ruth closely for another long moment, then sighed.

'All is well. She has gone into deeper sleep. I want her waking to be smooth and gentle, but for now, we can let her go. Unless she is shaken, nothing will disturb her.'

She lifted the girl back onto the grass and spread her own cloak over her. A guardianship, Magnus guessed, and possibly even another sleep charm.

'How did you do that?' he asked, as she scrambled to her feet, facing the gathering riders. 'Lifting her in the way you did. She is as tall as you.'

'The will and the Holy Mother make many things possible.' Elfrida held out both hands to help him up, laughing as he rose without her aid.

'All is well,' she said a second time. 'Magnus . . . she is untouched as yet.'

He nodded, a shiver skidding over him as he recollected the chilling words, *She left because she was not going to be first.*

'Ruth will recover more quickly because she is innocent.'

Pray God we reach the others in time, especially the first. Magnus nodded again.

'Excellent,' he said. 'Though I like it not that Ruth and Rowena are small.' *Like you.*

Elfrida said quietly, 'I am too old for Silvester.'

'That may be true, but I still do not like it.'

'Ruth recognizes you as a friend,' his wife went on quickly. 'You kept her safe as she flew in dreams. She heard your vow to guide her home. She will not forget.'

'Good.' *If that means she does not shriek on seeing me afresh, I am content.* Magnus spotted Lady Astrid through a haze of dust, a thunder of horses. 'Here is another 'friend'. What do we tell her?'

'Enough, but not too much,' replied

Elfrida, repinning her veil and raising her chin. 'She, rather, has things she should tell us.'

'Amen,' said Magnus.

9

As Lady Astrid dismounted, Elfrida glanced again at Magnus. 'Did you find any trace of the other missing girls?' she asked quickly. Her husband frowned and shook his head, once. She felt aggrieved herself.

There should be some signs of Silvester. He is a man, yet he seems to come and go like a spirit. Is he another dark wizard? I sense not, but what if I am mistaken? What is amiss, too, with Magnus? Why is he so irritated with me, so restrained? What have I done?

And here, striding forward with a face as rigid as a steel blade, was Rowena's 'guardian', and a paltry one to Elfrida's way of thinking. *The lady rides to our manor from here and then rides back. Why? Why does she travel in person when she could send messengers? Does she care so much?*

113

No, but she does not want to give up control. She does not trust anyone. Since I rode out in haste she assumes there must be news, so sets out herself. She wants to be on hand to react.

'Looks like an icicle,' Magnus muttered against her ear. Aloud he said, 'Lady Astrid, you come at a lucky moment. I have good tidings — not so fast, young man.'

A squire was trying to make for the sleeping girl. Before Elfrida could react, Magnus stepped in front of the youth and stopped him from shoving past the rest of Lady Astrid's maids and attendants. 'The lass needs peace.'

Pale as a frozen primrose, Lady Astrid yanked the squire aside. 'For shame! You deny me a reunion with my ward?'

'No indeed, my lady, but this girl is not Rowena.' Magnus held up a hand before Lady Astrid could protest. 'She knows your ward, though. From her my wife has learned that Rowena is alive and unharmed.'

'For now,' put in Elfrida, wanting the

woman to face her. 'The girl who sleeps, her name is Ruth. She and Rowena were taken by a man called Silvester.'

Lady Astrid's expression did not change, but her eyes widened. She turned abruptly to Magnus. 'Where is he?' she demanded.

'We should know soon enough. We have learned — '

'*Mon Dieu!* Rouse the girl, compel her to talk!'

'Ruth does not know.' Before Magnus could stop her, Elfrida stepped directly in front of Lady Astrid. 'Her recollections are cloudy. Silvester drugged her with a tincture of the eastern poppy.'

'An expensive potion,' Magnus threaded in seamlessly, understanding the thrust of her conversation. 'One beyond the reach and purses of all but the very rich and powerful, the *Norman* rich and powerful — like the sweets Silvester feeds them.'

The lady disguised the tiny start she made then by tweaking the folds of her long cloak. 'How does this serve?' she snapped. 'You, sir, are meant to be a tracker. Why have you not found my ward?'

Magnus looked as genial as he ever could with his scars, and his reply sounded mild but was to the heart. 'You delayed in seeking my help, Lady Astrid. You also gave me no trace of the other victims.'

'Though you surely had it. Gifted to you by anxious, trusting parents.' With that insight, Elfrida appreciated more. Curbing a livid flash of temper, she said, 'Had you not been so single-minded and selfish in your search, you might have recovered Rowena with the other girls.'

She heard a restive shuffling among the followers of the lady and knew they agreed.

'Silvester is not, as you have it, a traveling player,' Magnus remarked quietly.

'Nor a Jew, as you also told us. As you lied to us,' said Elfrida.

Lady Astrid said nothing.

'We know he is handsome,' Elfrida went on. 'We know he has a covered wagon that he uses to lure the young maids he wants. Sometimes he takes a girl along with him, to show favor and to beguile other victims.'

Magnus slapped his hand against his thigh. 'So he seems safe to them,' he said. 'Of course.'

'He plays the pipes to soothe,' Elfrida said, this time watching Lady Astrid's maids. Githa stared at the ground. Seeing her through the eyes of the spirit world, Elfrida saw Githa's panic as a dark nimbus around the young woman's perfectly groomed head. *I must talk to her alone. She does know this stranger, of that I am sure.* With any luck, Githa would later seek her out.

'These excuses serve no purpose. You have not found Rowena.' Lady Astrid attacked again.

'And you have not told us the whole story, Madam, so we are quit.'

Lady Astrid tried to stare down her nose at the taller, sinewy Magnus but could not. 'I do not owe you any explanation,' she began, but he glared at her and she fell silent.

'Someone should explain,' he commanded. 'Or I am done here.'

''Fore God, my lady, say for Rowena!' shouted one of her men, instantly stopping as Lady Astrid swept about to skewer the speaker with a glance.

'I will.' Leading his own pony and Apple, Rowena's bay, Tancred nudged through the knot of older men and maids. Elfrida marked how they made way for him. The boy looked determined, older than his years. He launched into a spate of Norman French.

'English, if you please,' said Magnus. 'Have you found Ruth's mother and kindred and told them that she is safe?'

Tancred scowled and began afresh in English. 'They know. Your men told them. Her mother is walking over. I rode ahead.'

He stopped, perhaps realizing how cold that sounded. Elfrida could only hope he realized it.

Magnus certainly did. 'A true knight, to leave a widowed mother plodding in your dust. Go on.'

The boy's shoulders slumped for an instant and then he spoke, his voice a little shrill and his words very formal, as if learned by rote. 'Rowena Gifford is now the sole heir of William the Fair. Her father intended her for the church, but that was not Rowena's wish. She and I plighted our troth many years ago, when we were children. Father Jerome witnessed our vow.'

'That fellow is everywhere,' remarked Magnus, 'And another who seems to believe that truth is a feast he need only pick at, that he may choose to share what he likes.'

'How do you know that her father is dead?' Elfrida asked.

'Because he is also a Percival, one of the sons of the overlord of the late William the Fair. You are, Tancred, are you not?' Magnus challenged, his brown eyes burning very dark. 'One of your names may be Olafsson but you are also a Percival. These great families take great interest in land and who owns it.'

In Tancred's rapid glance to Lady Astrid, Elfrida appreciated the rest. 'And the Lady Astrid is also a Percival by birth and a Gifford by marriage.' She ignored the noble woman's hiss of displeasure. 'You two know each other.'

'Of course,' Tancred answered, with a shrug. 'She is my aunt.'

The open, careless way he admitted this proved more to Elfrida. Lady Astrid was also Tancred's ally and advocate. The lady confirmed it by confessing, 'Tancred is my godson.'

'But Tancred is not the only Percival keen to win Rowena's hand in any future marriage, especially now she is an heiress,' Magnus added shrewdly. 'Hence your lack of truth, my lady, to Elfrida and myself, and your clumsy plotting. You fear powerful rivals in your quest to bring these youngsters together.'

Tight-lipped, her face crimsoning to an unbecoming red, Lady Astrid said, 'These matters should be private.'

'No, they should not,' said Elfrida at once. 'Too much has already been done in secret, and for too long.'

Sensing eyes on her, she turned and saw Githa, as pale as her lady was scarlet. *There are still more secrets here, new secrets. Has Lady Astrid promised her ward to another, as well as to Tancred? Is this why the girl had to vanish, so the lady could negotiate for a richer dowry and terms, have two nobles contesting for Rowena and her lands?*

If Tancred is telling the truth, then Lady Astrid must know that Rowena would go with Tancred. But now she cannot do so. Was this why she was taken, to stop her from joining her betrothed?

All the time, the other maids had been kidnapped and these nobles knew and did nothing.

'Who is Silvester, Lady Astrid?' she asked aloud. 'I think you know very well.'

★ ★ ★

Sorely tempted to roar at the Norman icicle and the lad Tancred, to compel them to talk, Magnus felt a narrow hand grip firmly around his wrist. Elfrida murmured, 'Step back, my love,' and pulled.

Intrigued, aware of a slight tingle against his sun-baked neck, Magnus stepped with her.

'Fall away,' she said aloud.

Everyone took a backward stride, though Magnus was too proud to be astonished at this piece of magic. *My witch-wife knows something.* At the edge of the tiny circle that had opened in the jostling crowd, he saw Lady Astrid's haughty bewilderment.

'What?' she mouthed in French, but had no chance to complain. Before any could react — *except for my Elfrida* — an arrow buried itself with a thud in the middle of the open circle.

'No more,' said Elfrida, calm while those around her were fluttering and flapping their hands, Lady Astrid still mouthing French and her maids uttering tiny cries of distress. 'It is a message. See the red and gold streamers? Those colors mean something. If the archer had hit any of us he would have been sorry.'

She scowled, her amber eyes as brilliant and piercing as a falcon's. Magnus sensed her mounting disgust as she added, 'It would have been a mistake.'

'Maybe, though a shout or trumpet call would have served as well.' Magnus stepped forward and plucked the arrow and its streamers out of the ground, but Elfrida was already moving.

'They meant it as both message and threat,' she tossed over her shoulder. 'Let me pass, please.'

The stuttering crowd parted, then she was running, with Magnus racing after her. They reached the sleeping Ruth together and stood before her.

This child sleeps still and Elfrida looks as grim as she ever can.

Magnus checked his weapons and stared along the road, where a boiling cloud of dust betrayed new riders. A scampering behind them signaled that

Tancred, Lady Astrid and their people had also read the streamers and were hurrying to meet whoever was coming.

'Unless I am mistaken, the colors attached to the arrow are those of the Percivals,' Magnus said quietly. 'It is a small troop, so they dare not attack.'

Squinting her eyes into the fierce sun, Elfrida nodded. 'They wish to parley, or have a spoken message to deliver. One or 't'other, though I am not sure which.'

Gripping his sword hilt, Magnus did not greatly care. 'Now we shall have answers, at least.' *I shall get them at sword's point, if need be.*

Slim and straight beside him, Elfrida sighed. 'I doubt that we shall like them.'

10

The herald was a Percival. A bastard Percival, but Master Oswin knew his due. Once he had stepped down from his horse, the Lady Astrid and then the Lord Tancred should have greeted him. Instead, a rough, hideously mangled country knight strode forward and growled in English, 'Keep your men back. What terms from Silvester?'

'You have no courtesy, sir!' Oswin flared. He gasped as a steel blade knocked against his shoulder and the rough knight spoke again, his words dropping like stones.

'Do not talk to me of fine manners. Splendor in Christendom, man, you could have hit anyone with that loosed arrow! Worse, you fired at my wife. Do not dare tell me I should be pleased.'

Oswin stared down the long sword point into a dark devil's face and felt his bowels turn to water. His party had stopped on the road, leaving him exposed. Above his own ragged breathing, Oswin heard the scarred knight.

'Speak to me of manners when your kindred act as true lords and save the lasses who have been taken. Now, what terms?'

'We know where your lands and manor — ' Faster than an adder, the sword lay against Oswin's neck. The rest of his proud speech suffocated in his throat.

'Never make threats that you cannot make good. I am a crusader who fought at Azaz. I have waded through blood.'

Standing beside this towering, bestial figure, a plain-clothed wren of a girl stared through Oswin's skull as if she knew his thoughts.

'He does not come from Silvester,' she remarked in English. 'Though he knows him.'

She smiled and Oswin recognized how beautiful she was, with her sweet face and her long red hair. Despite his sweating terror, he felt soothed.

'At your service,' he mumbled, conscious of the beast-knight's sword still nibbling his neck.

'Come, Master Oswin, can we not help each other?' Inviting a response, the girl lifted her delicate hands. 'You are from . . . ?'

How does she know my name? 'I am the herald of Sir Richard de Coucy.'

The wench widened a pair of sparkling golden-brown eyes and, to please her, Oswin found himself adding, 'My lord is the elder brother of the young lord Tancred.'

'No brother of mine!' Tancred flung himself closer. 'He wants Rowena! She was betrothed to me first!'

'Family quarrels are always the worst,' remarked the ugly knight. It was impossible to tell if he smiled or scowled, but he lifted his sword from Oswin's naked throat and sheathed it. 'Say on, Tancred. This is useful.'

Tancred said nothing. The young woman, meanwhile, glanced at Lady Astrid, giving Oswin the strange idea that she even knew that lady's plans. He rubbed at his grazed neck.

'My Lord Richard offers his manor as a place of parley,' he said quickly, before Tancred raised another complaint or the comely redhead beguiled him into a further confession.

'Let your noble lord come here to Warren Bruer,' the louring knight answered. 'We shall meet in the church. Let the families of the missing girls be summoned. Have the priest stand as surety for all.'

'Will Father Jerome wish to do this, Magnus?' asked the young woman.

'If he wants peace with me, he will,' came back the brusque response. 'The fellow lied to us.'

'By silence only,' said Lady Astrid, speaking for the first time.

'Unlike you, then, my lady, but as my Elfrida says, there has been rather too much silence.' Magnus slapped Oswin so heartily on his back that the herald almost stumbled. 'Go back to your lord. We shall wait for your return and his appearance.'

'I shall go with you,' said Lady Astrid.

'And I.' Tancred moved closer to his aunt.

Oswin dared not take such terms back to Lord Richard, nor have his lord's quarrelsome family ride along with him. 'That will not do.'

'Aye, I thought it would not.' Magnus folded his arms across his chest. 'What surety can you provide me with, herald? We might ride into a trap.'

'The Lord Tancred, the Lady Astrid to remain with your men.'

'No!' bawled Tancred, while the lady looked pained.

'What else?' demanded Magnus.

Reluctantly — his lord had ordered him to offer this only if nothing else was deemed acceptable — Oswin tapped the pouch attached to his belt. 'I am further instructed to give you the holy relic of the Virgin, her bridal coronet, for your men to keep as hostage with my lord's brother and aunt.'

He untied the pouch and displayed

the relic, turning it so the crown's many jewels sparkled in the sunlight.

Many gasped at the sight of this sacred object, but the man, Magnus, merely looked at the girl, Elfrida. She said something in a language that Oswin did not understand, but however she answered, Magnus held out his hand.

'Done, master herald. Now let us be going.'

★   ★   ★

Of course it was not so smooth or simple. Magnus did not expect it to be. Elfrida would not leave Ruth until the girl's mother had arrived. Then she would not go until Ruth had stirred, which the child did at once when Elfrida touched her hand. Then Ruth had to have eaten and drunk something. After that, Magnus had found himself promising that Mark and two others would escort mother and daughter safely back to their homes on horseback.

She will make a good mother, my

Elfrida. Unless she does not wish to be a mother.

More instructions followed for a bemused-looking Mark, then finally Magnus lifted his wife onto his horse and settled behind her. In a column of twos, the troop rode west along the cobbled road, cloaks swirling in the breeze. The haughty herald cast rather too many admiring glances at Elfrida for Magnus's liking, but his witch was not concerned by such trifles.

'I am most sorry for any long delay, Magnus,' she said at once in the old speech — *our speech* — though he chose not to be mollified quite yet.

'Humph! That would be more convincing if you had spent less time gossiping with Ruth.'

'Talking, Husband — '

'Still, she almost smiled at me just now instead of screaming, so that is progress and all to the good. Did you learn more from your talk?'

She twisted about in the saddle to look up at him and he, used to her antics while on horseback, gripped her legs firmly with his so she did not fall. His horse, also accustomed to this shifting passenger, whickered and pranced a step or two along the road, to remind her to attend.

Elfrida, not at all disconcerted, laughed at them both. 'We spoke of food and midsummer. You were beside us and heard.'

'Even so.'

'Yes.' The brief merriment in her face faded. She turned slightly, looking straight forward between the horse's ears, and spoke over the beast's steady canter. 'He is very close but well hidden. That is why I asked after food. A local dish may show us where he is. Ruth's memories are scattered, a few images only. Corncockle flowers and meadowsweet. A pool. Red kites. Barley bread, a little stale. A soft cheese coated in brine.'

That stirred a memory in Magnus and he mulled it while trees and fields flickered past at the corners of his sight. This was good, rising country with lush grass, a land for sheep and well-tended pea and barley crops. Elfrida was right. Silvester was camped close. *If I can just remember the name of the cheese, the place where it is made, I shall know where to search next.*

He hoped the parley would give him some new insights, but in truth he had little hope. If this encounter at least confirmed his and Elfrida's suspicions concerning Silvester, that would be a start.

'Why is Lady Astrid riding with us?'

His wife's very direct question broke into his welter of thoughts. Magnus tightened his grip on the reins, staring at the straight-backed woman cantering directly in front of them, handling her fiery mount with ease. 'She feigns a sudden illness well, does she not? And recovers in a miraculous fashion. But to say truth, I am glad she came with us rather than remaining behind and beguiling my men. As for being a hostage short, Mark has the relic and Lord Richard will want that returned with all its gems.'

'The relic returned but not Tancred? His own brother?'

He sensed her bewildered indignation and agreed with her. ''Tis a grim business, I know, but Richard and Tancred are rivals for Rowena.'

'Yet surely Lord Richard is already surrounded by lands and goods!'

Magnus said nothing. After a moment, Elfrida murmured, 'Rowena is very beautiful.'

'So her present captor will not want to relinquish her, whatever the original plan.' Speaking in the old tongue in order to share frankly and plan ahead before they reached Lord Richard's manor, both of them were careful not to mention Silvester's name.

'That is what happened, is it not?' said Elfrida quietly. 'There is your hasty plan. Rowena's close kin die suddenly, she becomes an heiress and former secret betrothals look too small. But if she is spirited away to some place where neither Tancred nor the church can find her, she can emerge later as already betrothed, almost married.'

She squeezed his arms. 'He should have given her up by now. They, whoever plotted this' — Elfrida nodded to the riding Lady Astrid — 'must have expected him to pass her over to them.'

'A risky plan, since they knew what the fellow was like and his liking for young maids. They did not even arrange that he would see her first. Or if they did, they did not mark his excitement.'

Elfrida stiffened and he felt the rage boiling in her, anger as heat. When she spoke it was in a low, cold voice. 'Six others taken, also. Six. They did nothing. They promised and cajoled so their people would work, they took trace from the families of the missing maids so it would seem that they cared and still they did nothing.'

'The kidnapper is one of theirs, a nobleman, no doubt a Percival.'

'Tancred, as bad as the rest . . . '

That, he knew, hurt her. 'We do not abandon them,' he said. 'I promise you, we shall find these other girls.'

She crossed herself. 'Soon,' she agreed, clearly making her wish a prayer.

★ ★ ★

After that brief exchange the column accelerated and Elfrida had to concentrate on riding. She listened to the earth spitting and hissing beneath the horses' hooves and sensed the rolling tension in Magnus's big bay. This was a place of spiteful spirits and secrets, of sweet cicely bursting from rank ditches, of raptors preying out of cloudless blue skies. Was it any wonder the Percivals flourished here?

Gripping the bay's stiff mane, leaning back against Magnus as he brought his arms ever tighter about her, she allowed the passing country to seep into her.

Silvester knows every brook and tree of this land, as I know mine. He worships the white lady, the sacred Virgin and mother, and gathers corncockle, cicely and meadowsweet in her honor. Purple and white are her colors. He will want to have his maids arrayed in the same shades, perhaps for the coming midsummer revels.

Magnus and I must seek out dyers and flax workers and question them. Something else nagged at her, something she had known or been told and had forgotten. Even as she tried to remember, the memory slipped away.

There were the jewels Silvester gave to his maidens, too, although Ruth had shaken her head when Elfrida had asked her if she had kept any of his tokens.

She feared I would take the gem. It is precious to her, not only because it is gold, but because of the man who gave it.

Saddened, Elfrida fingered her own bright wedding ring, wishing for a selfish instant that Lady Astrid had never sought out Magnus.

And why did she? To disguise her own failure by involving and then blaming him. If he had recovered Rowena, she would have taken the girl back, and continued her plotting, playing two brothers off each other.

Is Silvester also a relative of hers? Surely he must be.

'Is she his cousin? His mother?' she asked aloud, appalled at the last idea.

'Hola!' Magnus's shout shattered her gloomy thoughts. 'What a place!'

11

The manor shimmered in the warm late afternoon light like a great tent in a breeze. Magnus counted two towers and twenty banners, two jetties and three floors, a great hall, two kitchens and a bath house.

Plenty of laundresses here.

'How can this lord want more?' Elfrida whispered. His generous wench did not understand greed.

'What kind of manners will they have?' she went on. 'I do not want to shame you.'

'Never that, my heart,' he said easily. He knew it was the snobbish poison of Lady Astrid that inspired his wife's fears, but part of him was disappointed. *Does she not realize by now that I am never ashamed of her? What does she fear of me, that I will repudiate her because she uses the wrong knife for her meat? And yet, are we not alike in this? I fear ridicule from my looks. She fears ridicule from her class.*

He hugged her with his thighs. 'Should you make any mistake, I will accept kisses as excuses.'

As he hoped, that made her laugh. A greater joy to him was the greeting given to him and his people by a crusty house steward. Already awaiting them outside the manor steps, the elderly retainer at once informed him that their chamber had been made ready.

'My Lord Richard bids you welcome. You have time to relax, bathe and change in your room before supper.'

'We have a room,' breathed Elfrida. 'So rich.'

'We have our solar at home,' he reminded her, but she was right. A private room for a pair of guests was grand indeed. The warrior in him guessed another reason for this bounty too, a hard-headed, practical reason.

The lord wants to question his herald and Lady Astrid in private first. That is what I would do. What I will also do is post my own guards outside our room and in the stables.

Then Elfrida and I shall take a bath, together.

'Excellent! Many thanks!' Magnus replied, smiling broadly as he dismounted.

⋆ ⋆ ⋆

Elfrida glanced at the bath-tub, then at him, a flicker of longing falling across her face like a beam of light, then she shook her head. 'I must speak to Githa. She knows more than her mistress wants her to know about Silvester. I must learn what it is.'

'Githa will be bathing and changing,' Magnus replied. He had his own designs for spending time very pleasantly before supper and catching the desire in Elfrida's face, he intended to see them all through. *In any hunt there is always waiting and this is our lingering time. I know, Elfrida, more than you, what will take that strain from your eyes and the frown from your forehead. It will also ease your heart and mine.* He rippled his fingers. 'Come, wife. Our bath will soon be ready.'

Still tense, she sped away, across the chamber and leaned over the wooden half-barrel. 'Only if the water is invisible.'

'They must heat it and bring it. While they do we will sample the bed.' Determined to keep her with him, he untied the bed curtains and drew them closed. 'The evening will be long and we shall need our wits. We should snatch a nap.'

Whistling, he danced across the wooden floor and gathered her close while she was still chuckling at his caper. Swinging her along with him, he had her back by the bed and bundled through the curtains before she could speak.

'Listen,' he said, blowing a kiss on the back of her neck as she seemed about to protest. 'Our bath-water. The first of many ewers, jugs, and buckets.'

If her ears could prick up like a hound's, they would have, he thought, amused, as she scrambled up on her knees on the bed. Scarcely breathing, her right hand half-raised as if ready to defend, her bright eyes traced the moving shadows beyond the bed curtains.

'Why do they not speak?' she whispered, when a slosh of water confirmed that the servants had begun to fill the tub and were gone for the next bucket-load.

'Nobles do not like their people talking.' He kissed her summer freckles, as many as he could, while she tugged at his belt and tunic, inhaling deeply.

'I stink,' he warned.

'I love how you smell.' Tearing off his tunic, she buried her nose in his armpit for an instant, then kissed down his ribs. 'When you bested Oswin, I wanted to do this and more. Salt and leather and my Magnus.'

Kneeling with her, he had his own delicious torment by now — whether to let her drag him flat on the bed and continue her warm, teasing kisses, or take charge and be her conqueror.

Since I want to get her pregnant I know what I should do, but she is such an appealing little wench when she is bold.

Still choosing, he dropped into the middle of the soft, spongy mattress, bringing her down with him. At once she stiffened, but only because the door opened again.

'They will know we are here, Magnus,' she hissed.

He kissed the tip of her nose. *Not so bold after all, but still appealing.* 'Never fret! No one shall disturb us.'

He heard another bucket of water being tipped into the tub and tingled his thumb down her cheek. 'Does it trouble you, sweeting, our being here? Or do you feel it should?'

She said nothing, but when the chamber door closed, she wrapped her arms tightly around his neck and yanked him into her kiss. Delighted, he plunged into her embrace, though planning to do things differently later.

*   *   *

Elfrida dozed. She and Magnus had made love in the way he wanted of late, like a stallion and mare. He was so deep inside her in that way, she was so captive beneath him, that she felt overwhelmed by love.

I am wanton, too, for in the end, when he spun me over on the pillow, I did not care if the servants were beyond the bed curtains or not. He had me then and I was his and that was all that mattered.

Dizzy with fully quenched desire, replete as Magnus — *my magnificent brute of a husband* — caressed her back and thighs and bottom, she drifted between wakefulness and sleep. He whispered to her, love words in the old speech, and praised her skin and lissome curves and hair.

I am glad.

But still the beat of her slowing heart had a sadness in it. *I miss his face as we make love.*

The thought pierced her, then was gone and she glowed afresh, aware that the bath-water was ready but far too comfortable to move.

I know we must shift soon and face these Percivals, but not yet, thank the Mother, not yet . . .

12

While he and Elfrida bathed, the unseen servants had removed his wife's gown and left her another, a curious thing, to Magnus's way of thinking.

'Where are its sleeves?' he asked, flinging his towel onto the bed as he stared at the robe draped over the window shutters. By the dim sunlight in the room it looked a faded brown. Missing sleeves and belt it was as shapeless as a monk's cassock, with a drab, short veil to match.

This is the ugliest dress I have yet seen and they expect my Elf to wear it.

Anger started to burn, a rage that tempered him both hot and cold, like a quenched new sword. Swiftly he unbarred the door and spoke to his own guards, a few crisp words in an old crusader code that only they would understand. Stepping back into the room, he asked, 'Where is the maid to help you dress?'

Surprisingly sanguine, Elfrida grinned, giving him a bow that had her bath-towel slipping in an interesting way and quelled his temper for the moment. 'You have no fresh clothes at all, my lord, so by those lights I have done quite well.'

'I doubt that any of Lord Richard's garb will fit me and they dare not give me the clothes of any other.' Admiring afresh his wife's lissome shape and her smooth, clean skin, Magnus shook out the worst creases and dust in his braies and tunic and began to dress again. Part of him longed to stay and embrace his naked lady, but the warrior in him wanted to hasten out of the chamber, seize the first Percival he found and challenge the fellow to armed combat.

'That will not help the missing girls,' remarked Elfrida quietly, in that uncanny divining of his thoughts.

'But you do realize why they have done this?'

'As a deliberate insult disguised as a courtesy, to remind us of my lower class? To shame me and disconcert you? Yes, I do. What I cannot understand is why.'

Her question caught his smoldering attention, as she must have known it would. 'Are we not their guests?' she persisted. 'Do they not want our help?'

'Perhaps not. Perhaps Lady Astrid and Lord Richard have come to a new, fresh-minted agreement and look to deal with Silvester themselves.'

'But only for Rowena.'

'Yes, and I would say that rag of a robe is part of their new tactics.' He belted on his sword and immediately felt more himself, more in control. 'By this slight, they say 'There has been a change of plan. A sudden change of plan, but one we like, because we do not need you any longer and we shall waste no more effort in attempting to charm you as guests.' That is what they believe, I vow. It matches their other hasty designs.'

'The Lady Astrid's plot to have her own ward kidnapped.'

'Indeed. Their mistake now is that they long to show it off.'

'And break sacred guest bonds to do so,' remarked Elfrida quietly. 'They are entirely too proud.'

'Elfrida, their pride shows a fatal arrogance. These are folk who are used to ordering 'Do this,' and it is done. They do not understand the limits of their power.'

'As you said to the herald, they make idle threats and are usually believed.'

He looked closely at his wife, marking her unusual stillness. 'Did you and Lady Astrid cross each other again earlier today?'

She nodded, toweling herself in a distracted way, for something to do. He lifted the towel from her and began to pat her hair. 'So there is malice and revenge on the lady's part in the giving of that gown.'

'Yes, sir.'

Her 'sir' and her nakedness stirred him anew, but, before he could tumble her to bed again, Elfrida hurried to the chamber window. Peeping through the half-closed shutters, displaying the narrow back and pert rump he had so recently soaped and rinsed, she nodded and turned back to him.

'There are flowers growing on the common land, tall, lush flowers. Will you gather some for me, please, Magnus? Enough for me to wind about my arms? The corncockle and oxeye daisies shall do very well and will be pretty.'

She smiled now, her amber eyes sparking with intent. 'Purple and white are Silvester's colors, so we shall see how my costume is received.'

'Sleeves of flowers and not a bud or blossom stolen from any land of theirs.' Grimly satisfied at her ingenuity, he started for the door. 'Admit no other but me,' he ordered, and stalked out to the stairway.

★　★　★

None stopped him as he stalked to the common land. A page, kicking up dust on a nearby path, carrying a harp, shrieked in Norman French, 'A beast!' He sprinted off as soon as Magnus turned. An older girl, dressed in as drab a robe as the one the Percivals had put by for Elfrida, dropped her spindle when she saw him and crossed herself. She did not pause to recover it while she hurried off, wide-eyed and gasping. No guards ventured close, which displeased him, seeing that he was still itching for a fight, but being undisturbed he swiftly had mounds of flowers.

'Do you wish for garlands, too, my lord?' remarked Elfrida when she saw them, her eyes sparkling. 'You have certainly brought enough.'

Before he could reply, there was a hesitant knock on the chamber door. 'Away!' Magnus roared. 'We shall come when we are ready!'

'These are beautiful.' Elfrida mean-while was lifting up stems of corncockle, of oxeye daisies, of lilies and white roses. She gave him a look warm with grati-tude. 'Truly beautiful living jewels.'

He smiled, to prove he was not

aggrieved with her, and watched in burning indulgence. Flowers flashed under and through her nimble fingers, a cascade of whites and purples, shot through with gold. Elfrida was charming them, using her magic to pin and fasten the blooms to the dull brown gown. In moments, as he leaned against the door, ignoring another careful knock, she threaded flowers into sleeves and made a belt of lilies worthy of Solomon. Her face glittering with concentration, she stripped the roses of their thorns and fashioned them into a crown.

'My lord.' A plea beyond the door.

'Hold!' Magnus ordered, his cheek against the wood.

When he twisted round again Elfrida was robed in her gown and plaiting her long hair. 'Splendor in . . . ' The oath died on his lips. At times his wife's beauty was almost unearthly, utterly peerless. *How?* He wanted to ask, but it was Elfrida herself and what she could do.

The brown dress was transformed, enchanted by the woman wearing it and her flowers. She was a living tapestry, her face that of an angel's, her unveiled hair brighter than a dragon's flame and crowned by white and pink roses. Sleeved with oxeye daisies and corncockle, belted by lilies and garlanded with golden marigolds, the sweet fragrance as she moved was rich as the summer itself.

There were even flowers for him, Magnus realized, as she secured a spray of oxeye daisies across his chest.

'Hey!' he half-protested, but she wagged a busy finger. 'Today, you are my lord of flowers. These are your banner.'

He raised an eyebrow, which she ignored, being concerned as ever for others. 'Your men, Magnus, do they know anything? Can we get a warning to them?'

'Already done. They will have slipped away and have our horses with them. If Lord Richard had more sense, he would have closed his trap first, not shaken it in our faces.'

Elfrida touched her gown. 'This dress?'

'That dress.'

'So we should leave soon, should we not?'

He nodded. 'Such as it ever was, we have overstayed our welcome.'

She touched the belt of lilies, bowed her head and murmured a prayer, then straightened. 'I am ready.'

'To it, then,' he replied, hauling on the door and laughing at the awe-struck faces beyond. 'To it.' He relished the coming contest.

★ ★ ★

Sitting at his supper table, Lord Richard, a stocky, fair-haired, brown-bearded knight, clapped his pale hands together when Elfrida, escorted closely by Magnus, entered the great hall. Staring, the lord jerked his head at Lady Astrid, who had half-risen in a jingle of tiny silver bells, and she subsided at once, sinking low in her seat.

'Their meeting did not go completely smoothly, it seems,' murmured Magnus into Elfrida's ear. Straightening again, he brushed her rose crown and a petal detached in his fingers.

He released the petal as if it burned him, and Elfrida hid a smile as she nodded agreement. Lord Richard had so fleshy, bearded, and red-nosed a face that he was difficult to read, save for the basic emotions of greed and desire. The lady beside him, turning an unbecoming scarlet in her silken blue and gold gown, was far more open.

Dislike, fear, envy, sadness, wonder, and displeasure.

'I wear the colors of this land in honor of it, my lord.' Elfrida spoke first, feeling Magnus gently squeeze her fingers in support of her approach. 'The purple and white, as you see, and your own colors of red and gold.' She touched her red hair and her marigold necklace.

As she did so, she glimpsed a thought from a mind that was not hers, a picture of a man as tall as Magnus and young-looking as herself, beardless and handsome, garbed in green. *Silvester, where are you?*

Behind his supple figure lay a field of marigolds, a distant castle, a wagon. She concentrated on the wagon, trying to see more, just a little more . . .

She had to draw a breath and the picture fractured, flinging her back into the present. The silence that had begun to fall like snow in the hall was now complete. In the midst of rushing supper food to the high table, the pages and servers had stopped, as if they were encased in ice. Elfrida knew that for the sake of courtesy she should have waited for the lord to attempt some form of welcome, but she did not care.

What grace has this man shown to me or to the missing girls?

Lord Richard blinked a pair of flinty gray eyes at her and seemed to recover himself, his pride at least. He said something in Norman French, but was swiftly stopped by Magnus's answering burst of English.

'Oh, please, do not trot out a word about betters. I have slain better men for less.'

'This is my hall — '

'Do not dare threaten me or mine.' Towering beside her, Magnus had no time for fine manners, either — the Percivals' mean trick with the 'gift' of her brown gown had seen to that.

'Where is Silvester, so I may challenge him?' he demanded. 'But of course, you do not know where he is, just as you cannot find Rowena.'

'Or the other girls,' said Elfrida.

'Have a care,' Lord Richard spat, his round face glistening as his eyes narrowed with distaste. 'I need only clap my hands a second time and you shall be cut down by arrows.'

'Your archers will not see.' Casting the doubt, Elfrida prayed for clouds, whispering an earnest spell within her own mind, a charm of darkness and flowers, a promise to the Holy Mother.

Please accept this vow, my lady, and I shall offer marigolds and honey at your altars throughout this midsummer, also garlands of sweet cicely and lilies.

The scent of the flowers spiked around her and the heavens granted her wish. Daylight in the hall dropped abruptly as the sun dipped below the horizon. She sensed the distant crackle of thunder on the fine hairs of her arms, a sign of power and magic in play.

Magnus unsheathed his sword, the blade glittering in the sullen air. 'I see right well.'

'As do I.' Elfrida stepped forward. 'My knife would fall faster than any arrow.'

Lady Astrid spat words in Norman French, her features revealing her speech.

'I need no weapon at my belt,' answered Elfrida. 'There are many kinds of blades.'

She touched her belt of lilies, releasing another swirl of perfume, and Lord Richard flinched.

Sensing the moment as well as she did, Magnus touched her shoulder lightly and nodded to the entrance of the great hall. Elfrida turned and walked out, her flower garlands rustling, the marigolds sparkling, purple and white petals falling about her like rare silks and jewels.

Sensing the whole hall bewitched by her progress, she clung to one of her protective amulets as she won every slow, careful step.

Please let him follow in safety. Please let my charm hold till then.

She heard a shout behind her, a war cry, and her spine chilled. She longed to turn, look back, though guessed it would be fatal to do so.

Please let Magnus be safe.

13

She heard a strong, heavy man striding behind her, then, as she tried to run down the outer steps of the manor, she felt his arms hook her right off her feet.

'No running,' Magnus warned, bristling a kiss against her ear as he slammed her tight against his body and carried her away. 'Never run from cowards. That is when they shoot you in the back.'

'What did you shout just now?'

'When I stepped from the hall? An old Viking curse I learned from my granddad. It seemed fitting.'

Relief, and the power that her spell had taken from her, made her light-headed. Around her, the setting sun was a glowing blood red, an unholy omen. Though she struggled against it, her vision was darkening. Blood thumped in her head and ears and sticky heat smothered her limbs.

'We should hurry,' she said.

Magnus whistled, a single, piercing note, a signal. She could not stop herself from shuddering. 'Forgive me,' she tried to say, ashamed of her sudden weakness, but her throat was dry.

He tightened his hold on her. 'My men are here. Not far now, a few more steps to our horses.'

The gathering night swirled closer, spiraling round into a single black point. She strained for the light, for her own sweetly whispering flowers, but saw and heard no more.

$\star$ $\star$ $\star$

Tumbling down into the dark, Elfrida dreamed of the Lady Astrid. In the dream they were outside the lady's manor, strolling within a garden. Elfrida tried to see if any opium poppies grew there, while Lady Astrid sat on a grassy bank that sparkled with nodding cowslips. She did not invite Elfrida to join her.

'Until I saw your tricks with the

flowers and the gown I did not know you were a witch,' she said. 'Is that how you got yourself married?'

Elfrida shook her head. 'Why the deliberate insults?'

Lady Astrid plucked a cowslip and threaded it into her blond hair. 'I have no idea what you are talking about. I deal with you according to our mutual status. I am a lady. You are a peasant.'

'True, but you and your kin have a strange way of trying to win favors and of asking for help.'

The lady tore the flower from her hair. 'We never beg.'

'Is a request the same as begging in your eyes?'

'You should be honored to be any part of our company.' Lady Astrid dropped the yellow blossom onto the grass. 'As for the gown, it was fitting. I suggested it to my cousin. I wanted to show you as you really are to everyone.'

'Why?'

'Because your peasant arrogance offends me. But now I understand. You are a witch who has bewitched your country knight into marrying you.' She smiled and brushed the rich silk of her blue gown. 'What happens when the magic wears off?'

She is a malicious fool, Elfrida told herself, but it made no difference. The scene changed. She was back at Magnus's manor and a mass of armed and mounted knights were charging at the house. Lady Astrid materialized beside her. She wore full armor. Her chain mail sparkled in the blazing sun.

'What are your orders, peasant? How do we stop them?'

The earth shuddered beneath Elfrida's feet and already the noise of the closing horses and men was such that she would have to shout. *What magic have I to stop these horses? I charm and weave spells to cure animals, not harm them.*

An instant's hesitation only but the screaming knights were here, slashing at her with swords and clubs.

'You have lost your lord's home,' Astrid mocked, then the dream folded into a different space and time, a mid-winter courtly dance. Tall and strong beside her, Magnus whistled the dance plucked out by the lute players and offered her his hand.

I do not know this dance. I know only country dances.

'What are the steps, peasant?' Clothed in gold threaded with seed pearls, Lady Astrid passed in a scatter of rose petals and rose perfume, drawing Magnus with her. They danced to a dais. Colliding helplessly with the other twirling lords and ladies, Elfrida trailed in their wake.

By the time she had reached the dais, Magnus was already seated next to the lady. He frowned at her. 'Why have you not prepared the feast to my liking?' he demanded. 'These dishes are a disappointment, a disgrace.'

He indicated the bowls of stew and pottage, the simple, hearty fare that Elfrida had made since girlhood.

Magnus does not say words like disgrace. But would he ever be disappointed in me? In my narrow, local wisdom?

Learning nothing more, Elfrida started and opened her eyes.

'Good,' said Magnus beside her. 'Any more of that twitching and I would have shaken you awake. You were deep in a dream, my heart, and it did not seem to please you. Did you see anything?'

Elfrida swallowed and rolled onto her back. They were lying side by side on a bed of heather and ling, with Magnus's cloak draped over them. The horses were hidden, tethered amidst a stand of ash trees. Closer still his men crouched around a small fire and passed a flask back and forth.

'Nothing useful,' she said after a moment. *Nothing concerning Silvester or the missing girls, only my own fears mirrored back to me. And earlier I was not even able to talk to Githa. I have done nothing useful.* 'Where are we?'

'Well away from where anyone will find us.' Gently Magnus dusted pollen from her forehead.

'I thought we would ride through the night.'

When Magnus said nothing, she knew at once that he had stopped because of her. *I am a weakling who slows him down.* Ashamed, she forced her aching, knotted limbs to move and sat up. 'But the Percivals and the Lady Astrid know where we live and our people — '

'Never fret! Baldwin is riding to Castle Pleasant with a message for Peter. He and his men will go at once to our manor.' Magnus snorted. 'Doubtless Peter will think the whole matter an adventure, a chance to best the Giffords. He has never liked the family.'

She believed it. Peter of the Mount was also Magnus's oldest friend. *And Alice, Peter's wife, she likes me well enough, even though I am no lady.*

'Piers will be at the Templars' Highwood preceptory already. The Templars know me from Outremer. They will send men. The manor and lands and all our folk will be well protected.'

'And your own hostage?'

He gave her a piercing glance that instantly softened. 'You know, lass, that

I will never hurt Tancred?'

She nodded, relieved he was not angry at her for asking.

'He and the relic are safe. I spoke to Mark in secret before we set out for Lord Richard's. I told him to make haste with Tancred and take him and the crown away from Warren Bruer, to get back to our own lands and be ready to defend them. The lad may be bored and he may feel like baggage, but he will be looked after. After all, we are striving for his bride-to-be and will recover her yet, pray God.'

She breathed more easily, although conscience made her observe, 'Yet if the Percivals attack your manor, people will die.'

'Having the place stoutly defended will make them think twice. These men are cowards, believe me.'

He kissed her, a brisk *be quiet* kiss. 'We have no food tonight but shall do better tomorrow. My men's empty stomachs will see to that.'

'We cannot steal from any villages.'

'You know I do not allow that.' He kissed the back of her neck. 'Roll over.'

She felt his arousal and wanted to say, 'Can we not make love face to face?' but was too dispirited after her dream to suggest it. She wondered how she might explain, or at least seek comfort. 'Magnus, can we talk?'

He tongued her ear. 'You smell good.'

'Even though I am a peasant?'

He drew back a little, his face darkening. 'No more of these foolish notions, Elfrida. I do not like them and you should not heed harpies like Lady Astrid. Look at your sister instead. Christina is happy with Walter and already with child, as nature intends for all good wives.'

Alarm galloped through her. 'What are you saying?' *Am I not a good wife?* 'Have I done something amiss?'

'Not so far as I know, nor would I want you to. Now hush!'

'Magnus, what do you mean?' she whispered, afraid of his answers, afraid that he might stop his caresses.

'Later.' He flipped her onto her front.

He had been quick, masterful as always. She had given herself to him willingly and eagerly. Yet as he slept curled around her, Elfrida remained wakeful. They had not talked. Their lovemaking had been exciting and lusty, but she was uneasy.

Why am I not comforted? Why do I feel lessened?

The heart of their marriage was somehow wounded. Magnus had never compared her unfavorably to any woman, least of all to her sister. What did he mean about children and nature? What did he mean when he said she had done nothing wrong so far as he knew? Or was she making too much of her fears? *I wish my mother was alive so I could speak to her.*

One thing she did know. She did not want to sleep again and dream of Lady Astrid.

14

Norton Mayfield looked the same as it always did when Magnus rode past the church and fields and houses. A few of his people leaned on their hoes and scythes to watch the dusty column go by but most did not. The charcoal burners and woodsmen were busy in the copse beside his house. Goodwives weeded their gardens. The carpenter repairing the shutters of the kitchen block still sawed and hammered.

'How will I feed the extra men who are coming?' lamented Elfrida, almost falling from their horse as she waved to the children who played by the church stocks. Magnus snatched her back, spurred the horse into the yard and reined in.

'More ale, bread, blankets, and washing. I must check the bath house and our stores.' Elfrida counted on her fingers as she slid from the horse. 'Bandages, potions, the manor hedges and ditches. These riders need a breakfast now as well . . . What, sir?'

He blocked her path to stop her racing across the yard to the kitchen. 'Come and eat, Wife. The place is not under siege yet, nor is it likely to be.'

She crossed herself and muttered a charm, her forehead knotted. She was not like her sister, always fussing about clothes, although he half expected a complaint about that next. *Truth to say, her flowery gown still looks very well. I will not mention it unless she starts on again about how much there is to do. Scolding me then against talking of such trifles as gowns will divert her.*

'I know nobles, Elfrida,' he went on as she remained silent. He watched Mark run down to the manor's outer staircase and saluted the man as he approached. 'Come into breakfast, wife, and I shall tell you why Lord Percival is not coming here, not yet.'

She looked unconvinced but went with him.

★ ★ ★

Inside the great hall, Magnus discovered his hostage Tancred still at table, with Father Jerome alongside him. The pair were playing chess and picking strawberries and raspberries from trenchers.

'They have been doing that ever since they arrived,' Mark said in a low voice. 'Playing that game. The lad says he does not like the food but he still eats.'

Magnus nodded. 'Any trouble otherwise?'

'No, and no messengers.'

'Good! I half expected Tancred's parents to have sent some kind of word or threat before now.'

'A younger son,' remarked Mark laconically, as if that explained everything. Or did Tancred's father assume that the boy's older brother, Lord Percival, would help him? *If so, he is sadly mistaken.*

'Did the priest volunteer to come with you?'

'He did.'

'Where have you put Tancred's men?'

Mark shrugged. 'I left them behind at Warren Bruer but brought their horses along. They can walk here if they wish.'

'Any good horses?'

'One or two.'

'The relic?'

'Hidden with your book.'

I must look to my book again, make sure I am doing all right with Elfrida. Magnus glanced at his wife as she spoke with one of the servers. She had lost some of her pretty summer color and a few of her freckles. *Women often sicken when they are first with child.* The thought made him hopeful and indulgent together. He beckoned to her.

'Tancred will not look at me directly,' she remarked, when she joined him and they watched the two figures at the high table.

'His loss.'

'He must hate being a hostage. And we did promise to help him. He must feel doubly betrayed, and fearful.'

'Nobles are accustomed to being traded as hostages and expect to be kept safe. It is more likely that high and mighty Tancred feels he is not being held in sufficient splendor, or by grand enough company.' He flicked a glance at her. 'His aunt will certainly have told him that I am a middling country knight.'

'And that I am a peasant.'

'He had better remember you are my wife.' Magnus tucked her arm through his and escorted her to the dais. The priest greeted them while the boy managed a terse nod.

'Food first for everyone.' Magnus whistled for the servers.

For several moments the hall thronged with harvesters tramping in from haymaking and setting up the lower trestles, servers rushing in and out with flagons and bowls of pottage and the whole clinking of cups and knives as people settled down to eat.

Tancred scowled and jabbed his spoon into the central dish on the table.

'A guest does not complain about the

food.' Elfrida surprised Magnus with her frankness, but he understood it when she added, 'You are still our guest, Tancred. It is not our doing that you became a hostage.'

The back of Tancred's neck reddened, but still he would not look at her.

'Your aunt is now allied to your brother for her own advantage,' she went on. 'They will seek Rowena first.'

And I thought she pitied the lad. More, I thought I had to explain to her why this manor is unlikely to be attacked. She has already understood why without my needing to say a word.

'Richard will rescue me.' Staring at the table, Tancred spoke as if to convince himself. 'He will come and you will be his prisoners.'

Elfrida nodded. 'Your brother will not abandon you, but he and Lady Astrid will seek Rowena first. If they discover her, she will be lost to you.'

The cunning wench! She speaks to Tancred but also addresses the priest.

She shrugged. 'Of course, kindred are always very strong and trustworthy. You know your family best.'

Tancred's fair head jerked up. He glared at her. 'You know the obligations of family?'

'Why so surprised?' asked Elfrida gently. 'I know my loyalties here are to Rowena and the missing girls. I keep my promises.'

'As do I,' put in Magnus. 'I have not given up my search for them.'

Twisting round on his seat, Tancred seized upon this less-than-startling news. 'You say that because of Elfrida, because you dote on her! You would not care else!'

'I do not answer to you.' Magnus held his temper in check and kept his voice deliberately sanguine. *Hellfire in Christendom! Now Elfrida will worry that I spoil her. If I do, 'tis no one's business but mine. If any man here dares to say anything on the matter, I shall knock in his teeth.*

He waved aside Tancred's protest. 'I

will keep looking for all the girls because it is the right thing to do. Because that is what your brother will be doing, if only for Rowena. And because that is what I want to do.'

Sitting beside Tancred, Father Jerome cleared his throat. 'I believe I know where Silvester can be found.'

So the priest has changed sides again. What a surprise.

'You knew Silvester when he came to the church at Warren Bruer,' said Elfrida. 'You told Rowena she was safe to go with him.'

Tancred stopped breathing for an instant and reddened, but Father Jerome said nothing. He certainly did not deny what Elfrida had guessed.

'Where is the fellow then, Priest?' demanded Magnus.

Father Jerome picked up a chess piece, a pawn, and tossed it from hand to hand. His handsome face remained still. He was so even-featured that Magnus could not tell if he was disconcerted or not.

'You hoped that the Lady Astrid would help Tancred and Rowena to marry,' promoted Elfrida, giving the priest an excuse Magnus would not have supplied.

'Yes, I did.' Father Jerome looked at Tancred. 'The plan was always that Silvester would hide Rowena for a day or two, until word could be sent to you.'

'You did not know that Rowena had already sent him a message,' remarked Elfrida.

'Nor that my lady would change her plans.'

'Ah, it stings that she left you behind.'

Father Jerome's fist tightened on the chess piece but again he said nothing. Magnus was unsure if the priest had spoken from pride or injured feelings and did not really care. Either way, the fellow was clearly smarting. *And he deserves it.*

Beneath the table Elfrida made the sign against evil. 'A man who stands for Christ. A liar,' she said softly in the old tongue. 'A liar like Tancred, Lady Astrid, and Githa, and yet he is also a priest. How many days in our search have these folk lost us?'

Magnus heard her hurt and touched her foot with his. He could feel her heat and shimmer of anger, building fast. *Steady, little witch. We need to learn what Jerome knows first.*

'What did you say?' Tancred asked her. 'Were you talking about me then?'

'Where is Silvester?' Magnus repeated, ignoring the lad.

Father Jerome dropped the pawn, where it rolled off the table and onto the dais floor with so loud a clatter that the harvesters paused in their meal for an instant and heads turned to the high table. Magnus called out, 'Ale for everyone,' and the awkward moment of silence passed.

'Tell us,' he ordered, under the rush of servers and raising of emptied ale cups.

'It is a castle,' said Elfrida, adding swiftly to Magnus alone in the old speech, 'I have seen it in our quarry's mind.'

Tancred stuffed a huge strawberry into his mouth, as if to stop himself saying anything.

'Black cliff?' Elfrida went on, in English, speaking to the hall at large.

'Castle Rocher Noir,' agreed Father Jerome, with a sigh, hunching down lower at the table. 'Lady Astrid and Silvester both served at the castle when they were younger. She and Lord Percival must be convinced that Silvester is living there still.'

'With the result that Astrid and Richard have joined forces to parley with this Castle Rocher Noir — that's Castle Black Cliff to you and me, Elfrida — to hand Rowena over to them,' Magnus observed. It made a kind of sense to him, although if the master of the castle was unmarried or had sons, then Rowena might already be plighted to yet another squire or knight. 'Is this a new castle? I have not heard of it.'

Tancred burst into a spate of excited

Norman French, overwhelming Father Jerome's more guarded answer. Not that it mattered. As clearly as if she had spoken, Magnus heard his wife's voice within his head. *They are both wrong.*

★   ★   ★

Magnus forced himself to be patient through Tancred's increasingly excited descriptions of Castle Rocher Noir, and his chatter about its possible weak points. The lad was looking at Elfrida by now and smiling. *He wants to win her favor again before he asks if we can besiege the place.* Father Jerome meanwhile seemed to be trying to apologize, claiming the secrets of the confession as his reason for not being honest before. Magnus listened until the fellow paused for breath, then called for silence in the hall.

He rose and thanked the harvesters for their hard work. He told them that more of his wife's good ale would be ready at the end of the day. When the cheering had died down, he told them that his good friend Peter of the Mount was coming to the manor and that some of his men would need beds for the night in the village. Finally he wished them all Godspeed in their labor and promised that he would help with the coming wheat harvest. 'If any need us in the next hour, my lady and I will be in the flower garden,' he finished.

'She has so many flowers already!' shouted an aspiring jester.

On that note of laughter Magnus seized the moment to quit the great hall with Elfrida. Tancred and Father Jerome would have to wait. *I want to know what she knows. I want to know why she thinks Silvester is not at Castle Rocher Noir.*

15

The summer heat struck her like a great hand. Elfrida lengthened her stride and hurried beneath the shade of the apple and pear trees, whispering thanks to the Holy Mother for the swelling fruits. A bee investigated her belt of lilies, then buzzed away to gather nectar from the pink and white roses that Magnus had planted for her in the early spring.

He squeezed her fingers. 'Tancred will be chasing out here soon.'

'He wants you to attack the castle.'

Magnus brought her hand to his crooked mouth and kissed her thumb. 'You do not think Rowena and the other maids are there.'

'A castle is too large, too public.'

'For sure Silvester will guard them close, as a dragon keeps a hoard. So where? A cave?'

'Nowhere so harsh.' She turned and

sure enough Tancred approached, tearing carelessly through the rose thorns. She turned round again. 'What say you to a delay until Peter comes?' She prayed that Magnus appreciated she was playing for time, hoping to throw Tancred off their real intent.

Her husband stopped on the speedwell and primrose path, his expression hidden in the shade of the trees. His voice when it came was as bitter as winter and loud enough to carry across the garden. 'So Peter and the Templar knights understand siege craft better than I do?'

Appalled that he had misunderstood her, Elfrida reached for him. 'No, Magnus, please, I did not mean anything of the kind. If you will only listen.'

Her hands closed on air. He stalked away from her, long-legged and lethal, far faster than she could walk unless she picked up her skirts and ran after him. A stifled snigger behind her told her that Tancred had heard everything.

Mortified, feeling her face ablaze with shame, Elfrida passed quickly round the gloating boy. 'I must see to the ale.' It was the first excuse she could think of, one fitted, she supposed, to a peasant wife.

She stumbled back along the path to the manor house. Somehow she crossed the yard, aware that Tancred was not troubling to follow. *Why should he? I have no power in this household.* Passing a lean-to where the blacksmith had his forge, she flinched as a pair of eyes stared back at her from the shadows. She stepped closer.

'Aye, you never run from trouble.' Magnus leaned out of the gloom and grasped her to him, drawing her into the smithy. 'Did you like my indignation?'

He did not mean it! Relief was her first sensation, flooding through her, making her shudder. Magnus stroked her hair.

'You surely did not think it real, elfling? That was to give Tancred the idea that I am for Castle Black Cliff.'

'But you tricked me as well.' Hurt and anger began to dance in bright, dazzling spots before her eyes. She wanted to knock him over. Furious, she kicked his foot, striking the peg one by mistake. Every bone in her toes jangled and smarted and there was a curious tightness in her chest. 'You let me believe I had offended you and said nothing, even when I tried for your pardon. You walked away from me.'

He shrugged, petting her still as if she was a mewling pup. 'A moment's discomfort, Elfrida. Surely worth it?'

'You never thought I doubted your fighting skills!'

'Why should I?' he replied, maddeningly calm. 'I fight as well as Peter. I know it and so do you.'

'In spite of your wounds.'

His brows drew together at that. *Careful, Elfrida. He is not so calm after all.*

'Naturally,' he growled. 'And you have to admit it got Tancred off our backs for the rest of today.'

'And made me look a fool. Didn't you care?'

His caressing hand stilled. 'What?'

Elfrida was aware that her temper was too fierce. Perhaps she made too much of Magnus's dissembling and her reaction to it, but she would not stop. 'Once you told me that I was your equal. Would you have treated Peter so carelessly, or Alice? I know I am no noblewoman — '

The black look on his face made her stop. Slowly, as if struggling with his temper, Magnus breathed out through his nose. He folded his arms across his strapping chest. 'I have won us a day to seek the lasses without Tancred or that priest breathing down our necks. Tancred has just gone by without a glance. He'll be for the hall and more games of chess. He thinks we are not going anywhere today.'

It infuriated her that he was right, but still she needed to know. 'Tell me.'

'Tell you what? I grow weary of this complaint. You make too much of this.'

'Perhaps so, but I did not turn my back on you.'

'Nor I on you, madam.'

'No, you assumed I would trot after you, to beg.' The hurtful words were out before she could prevent them.

'Splendor in Christendom!' He yanked her against him. She felt his heart thundering against her ear. 'Were it not that the smith will soon be back from his breakfast I would deal with you here and now. Believe me, you would not like it, Elfrida.'

Another instant and he would make good his threat, she realized. Lamenting her lack of physical strength when pitted against his, she forced herself to be quiet.

★ ★ ★

How had they gone so badly wrong? Why did she think such things? Magnus did not understand. *I give her honor, feed, clothe, protect her, love her. We are man and wife. What else can I do?*

Explain to her, said Peter's Alice in his mind. *Lady Astrid and Tancred between them have made her doubt her place, not as a witch, but as your wife.*

Sage advice, so why was his head empty of speech? Elfrida was still in his arms and she felt a thousand leagues away. He ran his hand down her back and heard her sigh. They had this taut thread of sensuality between them — they always had it.

'Tonight,' he said, wishing that sounded more of a promise, less of a threat. 'We shall have this out fully tonight.' *What do I mean by that?* He did not know. He only wanted this strange war between them to be over.

Elfrida closed her eyes. For a terrible instant, with the tension yawning between them like a chasm, he did not know how to reach her.

'Why not the castle?' he asked desperately, keen for any diversion and conscious that time was passing. Every day the maids were held captive was a day too long.

Time is passing. Trying to force her scattered wits back into considering Silvester's likely whereabouts, Elfrida was aware of two things. That she hated this sudden rift between Magnus and herself and that, for the missing girls, time pressed. *Am I wrong, though? Has the distance always been there between us but is only now revealed? Look how we make love these days, never face to face. And what will he do to me tonight?*

Pushing aside such selfish thoughts, she spoke. 'As I said before, the castle is too public.'

'And this is a man who likes his secrets even more than the rest of his kindred do.' Magnus still held her but spoke without looking at her directly.

'He would be vulnerable there, too, unless he has a troop of men.' *See how carefully we are speaking to each other, Magnus and I.*

'To the lord of the castle?'

'To the lord and to Lord Richard and his men once Richard and the Lady Astrid ride to castle Black Cliff. Even if he lived at the castle before he took Rowena, Silvester will not now keep his maids where they can be easily stolen from him.'

Finally Magnus grinned and squeezed her waist. 'Aye, I see that.'

Relieved they were speaking more easily to each other again, Elfrida admitted the rest. 'Githa lied by omission when she told me that Silvester was unknown to her. She meant that they had not been introduced or spoken to each other, but she recognized him all the same. She knows his connection to Lady Astrid and Tancred.'

Magnus shrugged as if to suggest *this is old news*, but Elfrida ignored it. 'I thought her words strange at the time,' she went on, her voice quickening with excitement, 'but I had forgotten what else she told me until a moment ago. Silvester is interested in fashion and clothes and so is Githa. She particularly mentioned the dyers of Bittesby.'

Magnus whistled, understanding at once. 'You think Silvester hides in the town?'

'If Bittesby is where expensive spices are to be had, rich jewels and lush clothes, I think he will have a house there.'

'The cheese!' Magnus snapped his fingers. 'The cheese Ruth ate while she was with Silvester — Bittesby makes a soft cheese, coated in brine. I knew I would remember it!'

Excitement and a greedy rush of exhilaration, of hunting, burst through Elfrida. 'Ruth's other memory is of red kites,' she whispered.

'Town scavengers,' Magnus said. He clenched his fist.

'Bittesby.' Elfrida sensed its rightness even as she wondered at her own slowness. 'Why did I not think of a town before?'

Magnus was shaking his head. 'A town is the last place I expected Silvester to choose. Busy, loud, full of curious neighbors and houses with scant defenses.'

'And strangers,' Elfrida interrupted him. 'Strangers and runaways. People not asking too many questions. Neighbors who will spy for him and pass on the gossip.'

'Gossip, eh? So no need for stout walls. He hides in plain sight. Excellent! Bittesby town is but two days' ride away, maybe less.'

Before Magnus could move away from the shadows, Elfrida seized his arm. 'I must come with you, sir. You and I alone, I think, until we are sure we have found Silvester's lair.'

'Indeed?'

She did not quail under his frown though it was a near thing. 'Please,' she almost said, but she was done with begging.

'I have a plan,' she began as he shifted. When he strode into the sunlight, the rest of her words withered inside her mouth.

He hooked his hand into his belt. 'I

will not have you as bait.'

He understood part of her idea, then. *This would be only gossip-bait*, she wanted to say, but Magnus's growl stopped her.

'So small you are,' he said. 'So slender still. If I were only more a man, this caper of yours would be impossible.' His fingers whitened on his belt and he fell silent.

'What?' Magnus's frustration raked through Elfrida's mind like claws. As she stared at him, horrified, he jerked his head aside, checking no one was close. Her own feelings now raging, and even with all her magic she could not sense the rest of his thought. That was always the difficulty with magic and thought-sensing. She needed a cool, calm head to do such things and at present her thoughts and feelings were in tumult, with fear uppermost.

'My lord?' *What does he mean?* 'Please, Magnus.'

They marched across the yard in the same arrow-straight diagonal that Tancred had taken toward the steps of the great hall. Magnus snatched her hand and veered left to the stables, acknowledging the smith coming the other way.

'Are we leaving?' she ventured.

'Let me think.'

★   ★   ★

He thought while he saddled an older palfrey, a plodding beast who went no farther these days than a league or so. Elfrida handed him the reins and they both shook their heads at the stable lads.

'Come.' He had her up in the saddle before him, marking her girlish shape afresh. He had guessed it might fall out in this manner, Elfrida with a wild notion of putting herself in harm's way to save others. *She has done it before when we have joined together in a quest. But I never like it. Were I more a man, she would be with child by now, big-bellied as her sister. She would have no magic to hide her pregnancy and we would not be having this conversation.*

The shame of it made him burn anew. Peasants had youngsters. Peter and Alice had twins. *What if Elfrida wearies of her childless state and turns away from me?*

'I am too old for him.' Elfrida's words came between Star's slow hoof beats. 'The town gossip might draw him out of his town house to look, but once he sees me, Silvester will lose interest. And we will have found him without any knocking on doors. He will suspect nothing.'

If she dresses her hair like a maid she will pass as one for sure.

Tancred sprinted out of the great hall, saw the ancient palfrey and relaxed. 'Ride with us!' Magnus hollered, but the boy shook his head, clearly thinking they were on an amble around Norton Mayfield.

Sitting lower in the saddle, Elfrida hunched her narrow shoulders. 'He will not want to be with me.' Then, as if wary of being scolded, she added, 'I am not troubled by his arrogance. Tancred does not defeat me.'

Saddened by how she saw herself through the boy's spiteful mirror, Magnus wanted to comfort her, longed for reassurance himself. *Still, tonight is the last night of mating as we are doing, according to my book. Then she will be breeding and happy.*

Cheered by that, Magnus dismounted by the church. 'Stay,' he warned Star and went inside. When he returned a few moments later he found Elfrida exactly where he had left her.

He smiled at her. 'I did not mean you, my heart. I only passed a message to our priest.' She did not ask him what message, which he took as a poor sign. 'Elfrida — '

'Leave it,' she said roughly. 'We have scratched at each other too much already this day and we cannot afford to quarrel more, not when the safety of the girls are at stake.' She stopped and took in a deep breath. 'I know you will say that Silvester may have men with him, too many even for you to fight. I know I am not a noble or a knight who has listened to battle tactics from childhood.'

'I did not say that.'

'These girls may not want to leave Silvester. Have you considered that?'

'I have.'

'They will leave with me.'

Which is why I am even considering your plan, or a variation of it, though I dislike it intensely. 'Why the haste?' he asked, scrambling for more time. 'Another day and Peter and some of the Templars could ride with us.'

'And if you go with more men, your company will stand out. Silvester will hear of it and flee before you are through the town gates. What if he is not there but learns he is being searched for?'

'He knows that already.'

'But the girls, Magnus! Would you kidnap them again? Tear them away from a man who may be a monster but to them might be an angel? Would you only take care with Rowena?'

Part of him could not believe she had just said that. 'Elfrida, that is unworthy.'

She blushed, but he found no pleasure in her shame, nor in her mumbled, 'I am sorry.' He mounted behind her and rode on, every pleasure at their discovery of where the missing maids might be now spoilt.

16

Mark stared at Father Luke, his priest. The man had run from the church at Norton Mayfield and was red-faced and sweating.

'A May pole,' Mark repeated. 'For midsummer? Now? With everything else that is happening? Sir Peter coming soon and the Templars and the rest?'

'Set up today, in the road by the church,' wheezed the priest. 'That is what our lord wants.'

He spoke loudly enough for Tancred and Father Jerome to hear. Up on the dais of the great hall, the sulky pair had their heads bent over the chess board again, but Mark had no doubt they were listening. At least when Father Luke passed Mark a scrap of parchment, neither spotted it.

'To it, then.' Mark screwed the parchment into his fist and wandered outside to read. After he had done so, he passed the scrap to one of the servers to be sure he had his lord's message right.

He had. The server whistled and stared. 'Is he mad?'

''Tis as good a plan as another.' Mark also understood something else. This whole busy scene of putting up a May pole would throw Tancred and that priest off the scent. 'Elfrida is with him.'

'And we know how careful she is.'

'Watch your mouth, boy.' Sensible and concerned for their lord, yes, thought Mark. But careful? He and the server glanced at each other and both hurried for the stables.

★ ★ ★

Magnus nudged Star to the watermill at the southern edge of his Norton Mayfield lands, where the river flowed fast and bright. In the shadow of the creaking mill he dismounted again. 'Mark should be waiting for us inside.'

Elfrida nodded, wishing she could have this whole day over. *Time presses for the girls and why are we here? I wish I could persuade Magnus. We should hasten to Bittesby. But I have lost his favor. I should not have said what I did about Rowena. Magnus is no Percival. And what did he mean about his being more of a man?*

Dispirited, she slid off the bony bay and opened the mill door to a blistering fog of flour, a tumult of grinding mill-stones. She flung up an arm, clapping her hands over her ears as the ground shuddered under her feet. Magnus scowled, shouting something before hooking her up and carrying her through the mill into a narrow side chamber.

In this room she could hear again and the dusty flour was a little less thick, but it still formed a billowing cloud within the room. Dropped onto the dirt floor by her husband with no more ceremony than he might have released a bag of wheat, she coughed like a cat with a fur ball. Magnus smeared chaff from his eyes, cursing beneath his breath.

'How the miller stands this I do not know,' he said at length.

'The money is good.' Mark detached himself from leaning against a beam and approached. 'A fresh horse is tethered for you, sir, my lady.'

I am no lady. Elfrida bit down hard on that. She glanced at Magnus. 'A message through Father Luke?'

'It seemed the easiest way. Have you brought the clothes?' he asked Mark.

Mark handed him a parcel. 'Sir, I have two horses — '

'Go back, welcome Peter to the manor and tell him how things are when you get the chance. Keep a watch on Father Jerome and Tancred, especially Father Jerome. I do not want that priest getting word to the Lady Astrid.'

'Do you think he would try to or even want to?' Elfrida asked, thinking at once of Father Jerome's pale, sunken look when he realized his lady had gone off without him.

Magnus shrugged. 'Why should I care? Mark, I will take both your horses. We shall go faster with two, riding and guiding.'

Mark tugged on his red nose. 'I ride Star?' He sounded horrified.

'He is smooth enough and steady.'

'And slow. What do I tell our reluctant guests?'

'Tell Tancred and that priest as little as possible. Let them think we have gone to my wife's village.'

That will match Tancred's idea of me. Elfrida did not watch as Mark saluted and left by way of a low side door. *Why did I accuse Magnus of being like the Percivals? Now we are more estranged than ever.*

Magnus shook out the parcel. 'If we are to ride to Bittesby you will need to change.' He pointed to the green gown Mark had brought, her best. 'Do you need assistance?'

'No.'

'Let me help.' His face was grim. He

205

stood over her without indulgence, giving no quarter. She changed hastily, with faltering fingers, stripping away her gown of flowers and casting sleeves and robe aside in a bright puddle of color and fading scent. The green gown was tricky for her to lace, but she managed. Magnus did not touch her in any way. He drummed his fingers on a beam in time to the mill stones' relentless pounding.

'Plait your hair,' he ordered when she stood before him.

Silently she complied, weaving her froth of red hair into a single thick thread that bounced along her spine.

'Wear this.' Magnus held out the veil Mark had brought. It was very long and heavy, thick and black.

'It was my mother's head rail,' Magnus added. 'In case you were wondering.'

'Good. Not the Lady Astrid's.' Her attempt at humor did not make him smile. Was this how they would be on the ride and within the town? No more than civil to each other? *Is he angry because I am right in my plan and he must bring me along to Bittesby? Or is he still hurt because of what I said to him earlier?* Her own feelings were in such a quiver that she could not sense his or his thoughts. 'Do I . . . do I pin it right, Magnus?'

He nodded curtly and plucked a broad leather belt from the parcel. 'Keys and a purse are attached.'

She felt too shy to ask him to put the belt on her. Cinching the leather to her waist, she waited for him to speak.

He tossed her a sparkling necklace, a shimmer of gold and silver. *His mother's jewel.* Wishing he had fastened it on her, she wound the chill metal about her throat.

'There is a cloak. Will you wear it?'

Elfrida glanced at the black cloak draped over his shoulder and shook her head. She would feel buried alive in that. 'The day is too warm.'

He took a step closer and her heart hammered in her chest. She prayed he would kiss her but he merely tweaked the veil more closely about her face so that it hung down over her ears and covered all her hair. 'There.' He looked minded to touch the tip of her nose but withdrew, turning and stalking for the side door Mark had used.

Elfrida touched the veil, already feeling smothered by its weight. 'Do I look older, as you intended?' she asked, as Magnus was silhouetted in the doorway.

'We have a long ride,' was his only answer.

17

After the cities of Outremer, all English towns seemed small to Magnus but Elfrida was wide-eyed. Their ride to Bittesby had been fast and hard and he had expected her to be dropping with weariness. Instead she sat high in the saddle and remained lively, as if intoxicated by the new sights, sounds, and scents.

'Their gardens are so narrow,' she remarked, glancing this way and that as he nudged their horses through the town gate. 'But they grow many good fruit trees and flowers. How do they all fit in? There are so many people here!'

It was close to sunset and curfew, so the streets would be emptying, but Magnus did not contradict her. He wished she was not with him, that she was secure at his manor, but he was glad to see her interest.

If only her excitement did not give such a pretty color to her eyes and lips and face. He had hoped his mother's old-fashioned, heavy veil would make Elfrida look older. Instead, in some curious way, her gown, necklace and veil made her seem younger, as if she played at being a housewife. *The blessed thing is, this is my doing. I want her safe from Silvester.*

She brushed his hand. 'Do we use our names here?' she asked softly, flinching when a pie seller standing at a street corner bawled out his wares.

'My father's name was Guy, so I will be Sir Guy.'

'And I shall be Rachel.'

Magnus scowled. 'No.' He drew rein and dismounted, longing to tug her off the horse and drag her out of sight into one of the tall houses. He stared up into her glittering amber eyes. 'I have said before, I will not have you as bait.'

Her lower lip jutted, making her look still more youthful. 'It is but a name.'

'And if Silvester has a dozen men to

call from the taverns to set against us?'

She blushed, looking past him. 'Every second house seems to have a bush or branch over its door,' she said, mentioning the custom that indicated such houses sold ale or wine. Magnus went along with her change of subject.

'There are more pie sellers in the alleyways than I remember.'

Her smile flashed out. 'Do you also remember the goldsmiths?'

In snatches of conversation on the long ride they had agreed they should visit the dyers of Bittesby, the jewelers and spice sellers, any of the townsfolk with whom Silvester might have had dealings. Since Magnus had no intention of telling any of these people where he and Elfrida would really stay that night, he thought it safe enough to do this and see what they learned.

He laughed and pointed. 'No need to remember, they are right by the town wall, next to the gate.'

★　★　★

211

She was relieved by his chuckle and glad to be off the back of the horse. After a long day in the saddle, her thighs, arms, and even her teeth ached with the constant pounding of the road. She marveled at how fresh Magnus seemed and swore she would not totter or delay him. *He has allowed me to come, against his own wishes, so I must strive to be a good wife and help-mate.*

It was no hardship to be either. She loved him.

'I will see if the smiths have stabling for the horses,' Magnus remarked. He offered her his arm to cross the cobblestones, guiding the horses with his hand. Elfrida wet her parched lips with her tongue and went with him, fighting not to limp.

The goldsmiths, working out of doors on tables and fashioning copper and silver pieces rather than fine gold or jewelry, rose as one at their approach. The eldest, waving to the other two to carry the tables inside, greeted her husband.

A gracious exchange followed in Norman French. Elfrida was brought a chair and a cup of wine, which she shared with Magnus. The eldest smith smiled a lot and seemed agreeable, nodding vigorously at Magnus's horses and settling quickly on a price for stabling the pair.

When their horses were led away and a plate of strawberries was placed on her lap by another of the apprentices, Elfrida nodded thanks and glanced at her husband. 'Is it long to curfew?' she asked him in their Norton Mayfield speech.

'The watchmen know me,' the elder goldsmith assured her in the same tongue. 'You may take your ease, Lady — ?'

'Christina,' Elfrida supplied, aware of Magnus breathing out slowly beside her.

'Christina my wife,' he said now, 'and soon to be three and twenty. I seek a gem for her.'

'I would love a ring similar to that

you made for Ruth, my maid,' said Elfrida quickly. 'You remember her? A small, pretty red-head? She came with my kinsman.'

She listened intently, watching the apprentice and his master. Neither were disconcerted by her questions.

'A ring of garnet,' the goldsmith said, 'very delicate and finely wrought. Geraint made it for part of his master work. Yes, I remember. Your maid was delighted and Sir Silvester well pleased.'

We are making him another, was the smith's unsaid speech, whispered clear in Elfrida's head. 'Yes, Silvester said he was pleased,' she began, but the smith had different concerns from hers.

'Gold and silver combined, with flashes of garnet — '

'Have you any rings for us to see?' Magnus cut across the smith's description.

The smith scuttled indoors, calling to more, unseen apprentices. Magnus plucked a strawberry from Elfrida's plate and fed it to her. 'Christina, eh?' he remarked softly, with raised brows.

'Three and twenty?' she answered in turn, glad they were easier again with each other.

'Word will be spreading already round the town of our arrival. I want it known you are my wife.'

'Your *old* wife.'

His eyes crinkled with amusement as he ate a strawberry, quite unconcerned. 'Three and twenty is not so different from nineteen.' He did not add, though Elfrida knew he thought it, *And this way, Silvester will certainly not be interested.*

*   *   *

Magnus bought a gold and silver ring and necklace for Elfrida. He asked after dyers and tailors, mentioning a particular love of purple and white put together, and was told the dyers had their stalls inside the town and their workshops outside the walls, 'down by the river, at the bridge.'

'We shall stroll there before curfew,' Magnus said, clasping Elfrida firmly by the hand.

'You have a place tonight?' the goldsmith asked as Elfrida rose, clearly responding to his prompt.

'Either a bed at the Swan or the Bear,' Magnus replied, naming two taverns he had spotted farther along the street. 'I shall let Christina decide.'

'Most gracious, my lord,' murmured Elfrida, slipping her fingers free of his and pinching him. 'Where are we really staying?' she asked, when they were out in the street.

Magnus stretched his arms above his head and turned about as if loosening himself after their long ride. Over the wooden walls he spotted the meadows close to the river, with apprentices playing bowls and firing arrows at archery butts. Bittesby was so small they could walk there and to the dyers in less than an hour.

'A more private widow's house, along one of the quieter streets,' he replied quietly, and sighed. 'That is, if we can find a widow who does not shriek and scream for the watchmen at the sight of me.'

'Hush! She will not.'

'Hopefully, one widow will not scream at my gold, at least,' Magnus went on, marking the man-shaped shadow that fell over the drinking fountain across the street from them. Instantly alert, he watched how the shadow detached from the trickle of water and trailed after them as they moved. Beside him, Elfrida touched one of her witch amulets, then her eating dagger.

He frowned, disliking the fact that she had also guessed they were being followed. 'Do nothing,' he growled.

'Silvester? Already?' she breathed.

'Too soon to say,' he answered, seeing another figure prowling in a street parallel to theirs, matching their pace and going in the same direction. A scrawny ruffian with a straw hat tied to his shoulders shoved past Magnus.

And when he turns, it will be their signal to attack.

He lunged down an alleyway to the left with the sun striking directly into his and the followers' eyes. In that instant, while all were blinded, he pulled Elfrida into a house passageway. 'Go through to the yard,' he ordered.

She ran, stopping when a new shadow carrying the knife of a cutpurse blocked the low-roofed, narrow passageway ahead of her. Magnus grabbed one of the house struts, wrested it free in a shoulder-wrenching tear and moved forward to pass her.

Elfrida detected a slight shift in the air behind them — a new, more urgent threat.

'Stop!' she screamed and the creeping figure behind Magnus stumbled. Magnus turned back in the closed-in space and kicked the creature in the balls, leaving him coughing and crawling out into the alley. The straw-hatted man stepped into the alley side of the passageway, murder in his eyes.

Magnus thumped the house walls with his improvised wooden club and straw-man backed away and fled. The cutpurse waiting in the yard where Magnus had told her to flee was already gone.

'Are you all right?' he and Elfrida said together.

Magnus dropped the strut in the narrow passageway and she ran into his arms.

18

'No more tonight,' Magnus had said and Elfrida was glad of it. He wanted them off the streets and she agreed. Hurrying between the town wall and the house yards and gardens, Elfrida touched each door as they passed.

'Here,' she said, laying a hand against the sun-bleached wood of a tall, narrow corner dwelling and sensing a sad quiet within. Magnus knocked sharply and in moments they were inside.

Their host was not a widow but a spry, thin man who looked like a priest. From the tools scattered around the room he was, or had been a carpenter, but one with no wife now in the house to make him tidy them up. He smiled broadly at Elfrida, asked their names, raised sandy eyebrows at Magnus's scars but otherwise said nothing. He was glad of the coins Magnus pressed into his knotted palm and gladder still of their company. 'Alfric, that's me. I have enough food for us, or will have, and you can sleep by the fire. Wait! I have some sweets, too, if I can find them . . .'

Ignoring Magnus's plea to be easy, Alfric began lifting pots and pans from the fireplace, seeking the honey drops he swore he had made. Elfrida whispered a charm to help the man find them and closed her eyes. Her mind returned to the passageway and their would-be attackers.

Magnus could have been killed. A murder in a brawl was not a good way for any to die, leastways a knight. Sickened at the thought of her knight being hurt, Elfrida shuddered and opened her eyes. Gloriously hale and as alive as he could be, Magnus regarded her solemnly.

'Were they Silvester's men?' she asked softly, while their host had his back to them.

Magnus sat on a stool by the little

fire and patted his knee. Too shy to sit on him after their earlier quarrel, she shook her head, then instantly felt guilty. They were no longer sparking off each other but she dreaded that her harsh words were still between them. Needing to be close, she stepped to him and ruffled his hair. 'You had a cobweb,' she murmured, as an excuse.

'No matter.' He did not hug her as she hoped he might but answered her earlier question. 'I think those fellows in the alley were common thieves and purse cutters. They gave up quickly enough.'

'Bittesby is not as safe as it was,' complained Alfric as he stood on a stool to look over a row of glass and earthenware bottles on a high shelf above the fire, 'but no one ever troubles me here. Was it out on Broad Street?'

'Close to the horse trough,' Magnus said quickly — a safe enough answer as there were several throughout the town. 'Why is it less safe, Master Alfric? Do Silvester and the other town lords not care?'

Still without his sweets, Alfric stepped off the stool, gripping a pot lid. For an instant he looked bewildered and Elfrida said quietly, 'May I help?'

The widower glanced at her, entreaty in his faded eyes and face.

'May I cook and you and . . . Guy talk?'

This suited everyone. Elfrida slipped outside into the kitchen garden to gather fresh greens for the pot and left Magnus chatting with the old man. As she left, Magnus said quietly, 'Leave the door open.'

I am safe enough, she wanted to say, but reaction after their fight in the passageway had set in and she was glad to prop the back door. Building up the fire, scrubbing leeks, chopping onions, she saw Magnus and Alfric with their heads close together, Alfric drawing on the dirt floor with a stick.

He knows Silvester. Silvester and the maids are somewhere here in town.

'He has a house behind Broad Street,' Magnus confirmed later, while Elfrida shook and spread the furs Alfric had left for them on the floor beside the fire. 'The old man' — Magnus pointed up to the attic chamber where Alfric slept, already snoring after her supper of porry and oat pancakes — 'tells me Silvester is beloved throughout the town.'

Elfrida felt a chill about her heart. 'Beloved?'

'Alfric's very word. Last summer, Bittesby had a great pestilence of rats. Silvester, with his flute and drums, is said to have driven them out.'

'More likely the winter we had last year finished them off.'

'I agree, but the folk here believe in him, Silvester alone. Not the Percivals or Giffords.'

Elfrida shook another fur, aware she was taking a long time with their bedding. Magnus stood by the open door, his head cocked as the curfew bells rang out over the town. 'Do they hide him?' she asked.

'Not hide, so much as let him live secretly among them. Silvester has told them that he likes to be discreet, set apart from his more famous kin. The townsfolk lie for him. Strangers are told nothing. Alfric believes we know Silvester, which is why he talked. Although' — Magnus pursed his mangled lips — 'Alfric seems afraid not of telling too much but of showing too much. Perhaps he and Silvester have not always seen eye to eye.'

Elfrida thought of the widower. She had sensed mainly sadness and loneliness from Alfric, but she could see how her husband was also probably right. 'Not so much love between them, then?'

'I do not think so.'

'Do you know who lives with him? Silvester, that is?'

Magnus threw a pebble out into the darkening garden plot. 'I did not ask too many questions, or the old man would have been suspicious. But we know where Silvester lives, Elfrida! We can watch him. Tomorrow. Early morning. In Outremer, the time before dawn was always the best for ambush and for spying. Bittesby will be no different.' Clearly relishing the challenge, he slapped the doorjamb and turned in the doorway.

★ ★ ★

Pale in his mother's veil, Elfrida stared at him. Tension rolled off her and when he glanced down at the heap of furs she blushed.

'Kiss me good night?' He watched relief glitter in her eyes before she tucked her head down and moved hurriedly to him. *Shy and awkward, but she wants me as much as I desire her.* After their earlier clashes today he was both glad and sorry, glad she still yearned for him, sad he had caused her grief.

Take her. She is your wife. Magnus shifted restively from foot to foot. This was the way the Percivals behaved — one step further and he would be on the way to thinking like Lady Astrid and the rest of her kind. *They have corrupted me.*

'Magnus.' Elfrida tucked herself against him. 'Thank you for having me with

226

you today. I know you would have ridden faster without.'

He began to speak, but she touched his lips with trembling fingers. 'I am sorry. For what I said in the mill, Magnus. I was wrong.'

He kissed her hand. 'So was I. I would not have you so sad. I love you. Do you believe me? What else must I do to prove it to you?'

She flinched at his abrupt, raw question, making him feel even more ashamed. Without thought, only wanting to convince, he gathered her into his arms, tugged off her borrowed, black, unwieldy veil and buried his face in her hair. 'Never leave me,' he found himself saying. 'Never.'

Elfrida stiffened in his arms. 'Do you think I would ever abandon you?' she spat. Before he guessed what she would do she gripped his hair and, painfully, dragged his head up. 'I have left my kin, village and kind for you!'

She was witch-mad, he realized, her eyes slitted in fury and her face no longer pale but red. For an instant he actually feared her a little, but then the moment caught him and he laughed. 'What fools we are!'

Fools indeed. She had been as anxious as him. Her fury at his thinking she might leave him was balm. She muttered something in her own dialect and even tried to shake him. He tore his hair free of her working fingers and kissed her.

'Not that way,' she gasped, when they broke apart to look at each other. 'Please, sir, not — not — ' She broke off, covering her face with her hands as a long head-to-heel shudder ran through her.

'Hush, little one.' He stroked the tips of her ears, a tickling, gentle caress that made his own toes curl. He did not quite understand. 'I thought you, like me, enjoyed the way we have made love of late. Did I hurt you, instead?'

'No, never,' she said, and began to weep. 'I never see your face now! We do not kiss in our unions. How do I explain? They are good, lusty and I feel so much pleasure I swear I might die, but I cannot touch or share, only receive . . . I am not saying it right! Forgive me . . . '

'Aye, you are a passionate wench and no harm in that. Sssh, Elfrida . . . ' He rocked her, astonished and humbled by her outburst. *Feel so much pleasure I swear I might die.* He felt the same, but for her it was not enough. *I cannot touch or share.*

He felt her shiver anew and thought of his book. *If we do not mate the same way tonight, you will miss the chance to get her with child.*

What of that? Magnus thought. Yes, he wanted children, heirs and so on. He wanted Elfrida pregnant and happy. Children would tie her to him even more.

But tonight she needs me, not my seed. Whether for good or ill, whether it means I miss my chance of mating with her, she needs me.

What if you lose her later because you do not give her a child now?

Magnus dismissed the fear. It was

selfish and unloving. *Tonight is for her, only her. That is what love is, to give willingly even in the face of loss.*

'Hush.' His understanding pierced him. *No wonder that harpy Astrid hurt her so much with her arrogance, and made her doubt her place. In a worse, more intimate way I have done the same. Elfrida is a witch, my witch, and a warrior of magic, but in our bed she is a gentle, loving soul.* 'We shall be slow, yes? Very tender.'

Still a new wife, he thought. They had been married for less than a year. 'Will you guide us, sweeting?'

She wiped her eyes and nodded. The sight of her damp lashes tore at his heart. She lifted his hand in both of hers and kissed his fingers before she drew him to their bed of furs.

'Magnus.' She knelt on a wolf skin and he knelt with her so they would be equal. She glanced at the still-open door. By the twilight he saw her blush. 'Will you guide us, too?'

'I will,' he said.

He gave himself to her, allowing her to kiss, embrace, fondle, and admire. She nipped and tasted and tongued, at times in places she had never done before. He glowed and burned in the summer night, each scar a wound of trust, courage, and fellowship.

'The greatest wound you cannot see,' he said, when she touched and spoke of them. 'In here.' He tapped his ribs and pressed her hand over his heart, his brown eyes gazing into hers. 'Whenever I lose you. Whenever you are not with me.'

She shook her head. 'I am always with you.'

'Always you.' He kissed her, his mouth caressing, his brown eyes still holding her, his body warmer than the furs.

Eventually she sank against him, blissful when he wrapped his arms about her and covered them both with the furs. Coiled over his belly and chest, his body hairs tickling her breasts and stomach, the furs tickling her bottom, she slept.

★ ★ ★

The world shimmered with sparkling dew when Magnus gently shook her awake.

'Is it time?' she asked.

'Indeed. I have left more coins for the old man.'

Closing the door after them, they stepped out into the pre-dawn freshness. There was no need to speak. They walked through the sleeping town hand in hand, taking a circuitous route by way of the walls to the short alley at the back of Broad Street.

Magnus pointed their joined hands at a handsome two story house with a new jetty and shutters painted purple and white. Elfrida nodded, then stopped as a door in the house opened.

Magnus began to move back into the shadows. She dug her nails into his callused palm. 'Keep still,' she hissed.

A small, slim figure, carrying two empty ewers, walked across the cobble-stones to a well in the middle of the alley. As the girl put down the ewers and lowered the pail into the well, her hood fell away from her hair. From accounts, and her own dream-vision, Elfrida knew her at once.

It was Rowena.

19

Magnus guessed who the girl was from Elfrida's stiffening. And Rowena was beautiful. She had long black hair, blue eyes, perfect, even features, and a serene expression.

For all that she lacks fire, Magnus decided, when he could breathe again.

Beside him Elfrida said something in her own dialect. A chaffinch flitted from a cherry tree onto the ground in front of the girl, tilting its head up as if to admire.

My witch did that. Magnus did not know how he knew that, but he did. For an instant the flesh on his bones chilled to ice as his wife's casual command of magic disconcerted him afresh. Only for a moment, for Rowena released the pail and spoke to the bright, bobbing little bird.

Elfrida whistled — Magnus had

thought he was the whistler — and the chaffinch pecked its way over a cart rut toward them, with Rowena following. Step by step she came, soundless as the bird. He wondered how long it would be before she spotted them and screamed at him.

'What then?' he thought, realizing too late he had spoken aloud.

It broke both spells. The bird flew off and Rowena stopped, her blue eyes bright with surprise. She stared at him, then Elfrida.

'I know you,' she said to Elfrida in Norman French, her voice childish and sweet. 'Did you send my bird back to me just now? My finch?'

'Rowena.' Elfrida had no French and would not understand her question. 'Pax,' she added, using the Latin to try to convince they came in peace. 'Tancred.'

Rowena's slim black eyebrows came together in puzzlement, but Magnus thought that she even frowned prettily. More astonishing still, she had not called him monster or beast, or made the sign of the evil eye against him. *Brave then, or simple?*

'Tancred.' Elfrida said again, and she glanced at him.

'We know your betrothed,' Magnus said softly in Norman French, and braced himself. *Do I snatch her away if she shrieks?*

Rowena looked back toward the house with the purple and white shutters. It remained quiet, but for how long? *If Silvester has men with him, there may be trouble.* Was the girl signaling to someone inside?

Elfrida made the sign of the cross with her free hand. Rowena turned and faced them again. Her color had not changed, nor her countenance. She was still calm.

'Sir.' She spoke to him directly. 'My father had a knight like you, much scarred. Were you a crusader?'

Not simple at all. Amazed by this strange beginning, by their whole encounter, Magnus found himself answering, 'Yes, demoiselle.'

'I would like to travel to Jerusalem one day. Why is Tancred not with you?'

Elfrida did not understand what Rowena said, but she clearly heard the question in the girl's voice. 'Tancred waits for you at our house,' she said in English. 'I have your head-rail, too. The one you embroidered with daisies.'

Magnus translated, adding, 'Father Jerome advised him to wait for you at our house.' He hoped his mention of the priest would make the partial truth convincing.

Not by a flicker of expression did the child react in any way. *Wary. With her family who can blame her?*

'Rowena?' Magnus tried softly. 'We should not linger here.'

'Tancred should be here.' Rowena turned to go back but Elfrida moved first, releasing his hand and slipping across to the girl in a swirl of green and black.

'Did Silvester tell you that Tancred would come for you?' she asked, glancing at Magnus. Her words, translated into Norman French, sounded harsh to him, but Rowena shook her head.

'Ruth is safe,' Elfrida said, trying another way to gain the girl's trust. Magnus again translated.

'She has brown hair,' said Rowena.

When she understood what the girl had said, Elfrida laughed softly and tugged on her own flame-colored locks. 'This is the color of Ruth's hair, and you know it,' she said. 'You need not set traps for us. Ruth is with her mother now, safe and well.'

Magnus wondered if they were reaching the girl. *It might have been wiser to lie, tell her Tancred was waiting for her in the town.* But what then? She would want to see the lad at once and then they would need to lie again, more and more. *Elfrida is right. Honesty is the only way. These girls have already been deceived by Silvester.*

Rowena pointed to Elfrida, then him. Elfrida held up her hand, showed off her wedding ring. Rowena raised her eyebrows. 'But you are — '

Do not call Elfrida a peasant! Sick of

these Percivals and Giffords, Magnus stormed across the street. 'Elfrida is my lady wife,' he said, through gritted teeth. 'We came to find you and the other girls, to restore you to your kindred.'

'Magnus,' said Elfrida warningly.

'We cannot give you any proof, demoiselle, only that Tancred is about this high and this sturdy, has fair hair and an older brother who likes relics. Your Lady Astrid and Father Jerome set us on this chase. If you have any complaint, speak to them.'

'Magnus, please,' Elfrida beseeched, but he had not finished yet.

'We should move,' he said. Surely they must be spotted soon. He looked about to scoop both up, one under each arm, and bear them off. Clearly sensing his intent, Elfrida shook her head.

Throughout his rant Rowena had stood her ground, looking up at him through long, silken eyelashes. She smiled now and said, in perfect English, 'She is too young to wear a black veil.'

She laughed at his surprise. 'You are

so like my father's knight. I could goad him into marvelous indiscretions.'

Before Magnus could react, Rowena addressed Elfrida. 'I remember you from my dreams. I knew you would help me.'

Elfrida smiled and held out her hands. When Rowena clasped them she walked with the girl to Silvester's house, halting with her back to a wall timber. Magnus joined them, relieved to be away from the middle of the street.

So far so good? he wondered, but he could not say, not yet.

★   ★   ★

For one so young, the girl had remarkable self-possession, Elfrida decided. *Rowena is placid, not volatile, but I sense she will do little she does not truly want to. So why had she remained with Silvester? Time to find out.*

First, she rested her fingertips lightly against the door and detected nothing behind it but sleepers. She mimed this to Magnus, then turned to Rowena. 'Is

Silvester here with you?' she asked softly.

'Yes.'

'What time does he rise?'

'We danced for him last night. Usually he sleeps late after that, him and the others.' Rowena glanced at the ewers she had left beside the well. 'I never sleep so long, so Silvester said I might go out and fetch water for everyone. He is pleased when I do.'

'You like to please him?'

Rowena smiled. 'If it does not harm me, or others, I like to please everyone. Why not? Is that not how a Christian lady should act?'

She strives to be gracious, Elfrida thought, struck by how this young woman knew her own worth. *She is kind and Christian, but Rowena will not work against her own advantage.*

'Why have you stayed with him?' Elfrida hesitated, then said, 'Is it because you love him?'

Rowena shrugged. 'Where else would I go? So many of the townsfolk love and help him. They would give me back to him in a heartbeat if I tried to escape.'

Elfrida said nothing. Coloring slightly, Rowena said, 'My fifth cousin, Silvester Percival, he is not a sinful man.'

Elfrida forced herself to smile, though this whole matter was dark. *A cousin. She is a Gifford and this Silvester Percival is a distant cousin. No wonder Tancred was concerned about consanguinity. These two families are tightly linked.*

'My kinsman brought me here by a feint but he has not treated me badly since. The other maids and I are content for the moment.'

The words were brave but Elfrida sensed a certain loss, especially in the final, gloomy, 'for the moment.' *Did Rowena hope for more from Silvester, once she realized he was not going to deliver her to Tancred? Maybe for a while she did, but she knows better now.*

'For the moment,' she agreed. 'Will he marry all of you? If he chooses you as his wife, will they be his mistresses?'

Rowena sighed. Peeping into her still face, Elfrida glimpsed resignation and patience, disappointment and discouragement, but no real anger or grief. No real shock, either. *Why should I be surprised? This is a nobleman's daughter. Young as she is, Rowena is practical about betrothal and marriage.*

The girl's next words confirmed this. 'It is true. Silvester does speak a great deal of love, knightly love. He gave us rings and says we are his wives.'

Wives. Heart-sick at the idea, Elfrida suppressed a shudder. Beside her she heard Magnus curse softly in Arabic. At her back she sensed the sleepers in the house. *We cannot linger here too long, though. Time passes.*

'You share his bed?' Elfrida said steadily, fighting down an inner sickness. She felt herself sway and stars blinked in front of her eyes — tiny flashes of sheer, blessed relief — when Rowena answered easily, 'Not yet. Not until after the midsummer.'

An ancient festival and bridal time. Silvester wants to cloak his sin in a summer fragrance but he is still evil, a despoiler.

'The mother be thanked!' grunted Magnus alongside her, but Elfrida pressed her foot down sharply on his. Rowena was still talking.

'We wear the gowns he has made for us and we call him lord. But he never mentions marriage, real marriage when we are of age, at the church door, with a priest. As you say, how can he marry us all?'

'And you wish to be married,' Elfrida said, 'as I am to Magnus.'

'Yes, I do.' Rowena considered this with unblinking eyes. 'I love God and the church, but I freely agreed to be betrothed to Tancred. When I am old enough, I want a family and a home of my own. I know Tancred likes me a lot. He can be unkind and rude but I can manage him.'

Of that I have no doubt.

Magnus cleared his throat. 'Why not

come with us, Rowena? We can take you away from here and no one will stop me.'

No. No one would dare.

'You can be your own mistress. You do not have to do anything, choose anyone for a while, unless it pleases you.'

Bless you, Husband!

Rowena tugged at her left ear, a rare sign of disquiet. 'But Tancred — '

'You do not have to choose right now. Tancred will wait for you, believe me. He brought your horse with him for you to ride.'

Speaking, Magnus smiled so warmly that Elfrida felt pierced by a tiny elf-dart of jealousy. Telling herself to be ashamed, she schooled her face, glad when Magnus offered Rowena his arm, glad when Rowena took it. *She does not fear him. I am pleased for Magnus's sake that she does not fear him.* And Rowena was beautiful. Even Elfrida was not immune to the girl's charm.

Rowena finally smiled again and asked,

in a young, more childlike way, 'You say Tancred brought my horse?'

'Your pony, Apple,' Elfrida confirmed. 'They are both safe at our manor.'

Rowena clasped her hands together, her poise shattering in a flood of excited chatter. 'My little horse! It will be so good to see Apple again! I have missed him so much.' She flushed, as if that girlish confession was too revealing, and added quickly, to Magnus, 'Are your horses very big? I love high horses, too.'

'Come and see,' Magnus said, tipping Elfrida a wink.

Rowena took a step forward, then stopped. 'But the others . . . '

Her selfless generosity, so unlike the mean spiritedness of the rest of her kin, touched Elfrida deeply. 'We shall not leave them, either. Walk with me,' she said quickly, aware, as doubtless Magnus was aware, that the sun was boiling up the heaven and the town was rapidly stirring. 'Magnus, we can go back to the widower's,' she said.

'Aye, he will be glad to see you,

especially if you make him breakfast.' Magnus clasped her shoulder. 'Hurry along. I shall catch you up.' He dropped a kiss on the top of her head.

'Magnus?' Rowena was tugging on her ear.

'I shall accompany you and Elfrida. Then you stay with the old man. His name is Alfric and he is a carpenter, like Jesus.' He kissed Rowena gently on the cheek. 'Elfrida and I will return here and bring the other maids to you at Alfric's, I promise. We shall not take long.'

Rowena glanced at Elfrida, who reassured her. 'It is the safest way, believe me, Rowena, for you and the girls.'

Elfrida smiled as she spoke, though she was thinking hard. *We cannot take too long or someone may suspect us and get word to Silvester or to some of his sympathetic townsfolk to detain us. We have to return to Norton Mayfield soon, as well, or we shall have more trouble there. Does Rowena know her parents and brothers are dead? If she does not, when should she be told? Not yet.*

Rowena's next question interrupted her hasty thoughts. 'You will not hurt Silvester?'

'No,' said Elfrida confidentially. 'I vow I will not hurt him.'

I speak true, she thought, as she drew Rowena away and Magnus stalked behind them, protecting their backs. *I do not seek to injure Silvester. I intend to destroy him.*

20

Alfric was still snoring upstairs when Magnus guided Rowena into the carpenter's cottage. Elfrida had raced ahead and had built up the fire. Now she was scouring out a pot to make porridge for all of them.

'The gold I have already left for him will cover that and our breakfasts,' Magnus said steadily, when his wife shot him a keen glance after finding Alfric's store of oats.

Elfrida nodded and pointed to a twig broom standing by the shuttered window. 'Will you sweep the floor for me, please?' she asked Rowena. As the girl set nimbly to that task she beckoned to him. 'Could you break sticks for me?'

Breaking sticks for the fire gave them the excuse to work closely together and talk. 'How do we fetch the rest of the girls out of Silvester's?' Elfrida whispered to Magnus. 'By fire?'

'Too risky,' Magnus said at once. 'We might set half the thatch ablaze while they are still sleeping — and they sleep forever, due to the smoke.'

'Some threat of violence? Do not look at me that way, Magnus. I know it is desperate, but we do not have men or time for any kind of siege. It would need to be a pretend, false threat.'

'Real or false, they will bar the doors and hide.'

'I could tempt them out,' Elfrida began, considering charms she might use, but Magnus put his hand over hers.

'We both know what will work right well, and faster,' he said quietly. 'A face at their window. A hideous, leering face. A bestial monster, threatening to break in.'

Elfrida stared at the fire, feeling Magnus's sadness in her own frame. 'It did not work for Rowena,' she said, after a space, wanting to defend him against his own plan.

'And how many are like her?'

Still she argued. 'And Silvester? He must be out of the way.'

'Or even my good looks will not work to drive the girls outside? Agreed, elfling, that is another problem.' In his frustration, he snapped a branch one-handed with a loud crack and Rowena glanced up from her sweeping.

My height, my size, thought Elfrida, and spoke. 'Will you change gowns with me, Rowena?'

Magnus glowered and she added quickly, 'If he sees me as Rowena, wandering off, he will surely step out of his house to retrieve her.'

Suddenly Rowena stopped sweeping and pointed to the rafters. Above them, Alfric was peering down from the loft, his sleep-flattened gray hair fluffed out like a dandelion.

'Good morrow!' Magnus called up. 'We shall have a breakfast made soon, if it please you. Will you join us?'

He broke several more sticks at once and said bluntly to Elfrida, as if all discussion were over, 'Neither you, nor Rowena, are setting foot out of this house.'

★　★　★

Naturally there was no more argument, which meant that naturally Elfrida swapped gowns with Rowena after breakfast. The girl did so without complaint, merely stating that she would not wear the black veil.

'Quite right, child, it is too old for you,' said Alfric. He was busy carving a spoon for Rowena, having accepted her appearance at his house without question or curiosity. He took no part in the discussion that followed; indeed he appeared oblivious to it, merely delighted that he had company.

One good thing out of this blasted morning. Magnus watched Elfrida pin Rowena's veil onto her hair, carefully covering her red tresses. *If Peter were here with me, we could clear out Silvester's house by ourselves. Peter is handsome and the lasses would follow him for sure.*

Why had he not waited for Peter? Oh yes, had he waited for Peter, Tancred would be here with them as well, cluttering up the place, eating all of Alfric's stores and wanting to leave now that Rowena was safe.

'The midsummer solstice is in less than a week,' Elfrida reminded him quietly, though he needed no reminders. He watched her turn on the spot and check that her hair was still covered.

Magnus knelt and stirred the crackling fire. 'Why are we doing this? 'Tis madness.' *Surely I should ride back to Norton and bring my men, Peter, and the Templars to storm the place.*

'The simple plan works the best, my father always used to say,' said Rowena. She had stopped sweeping for the moment and now leaned on the broom, taking any sting from her words by granting him a sweet smile.

Magnus stared at her, while Elfrida asked delicately, 'Your father is Lord William?'

'My father was Lord William,' Rowena replied. 'My parents died last month.'

Elfrida's hands dropped to her sides. 'I am so sorry, Rowena.'

Rowena studied the broom she was gripping. 'I overheard the news at my Lady Astrid's manor. Or rather, Githa, who had been my maid, but who is now my Lady Astrid's attendant, she told me.'

Elfrida was nodding. 'I have sensed a certain division in Githa. I am sorry for that, too, Rowena.'

'Why? It is not your fault. It is the way of the world. People go toward power. That is why I sent Tancred the finch.'

'As a signal to come?' Elfrida asked softly. 'So you could finally choose your own fate?'

Rowena nodded. 'Lady Astrid and Father Jerome both told me that plans were in motion, that I should go with Silvester and he would deliver me to Tancred.'

'But you wanted to be sure,' said Elfrida.

Her words echoed Magnus's own thought and he understood very well. Dealing with these Giffords and Percivals, who would not want to make sure?

'Yes,' said Rowena simply. 'And I am glad Tancred heeded me enough to try.'

'He did that.' Magnus surprised himself by defending the lad but Rowena merely smiled again.

'He will know I am an heiress.'

'He still cares for you,' said Magnus and Elfrida, speaking together.

Glancing at his wife, Magnus could see that Rowena's continuing calm had rattled Elfrida as much as it disconcerted him. *Strange, that the girl does not cry for her father or close kin. Is she finished already with tears? Was William a brute, Rowena's mother another like Lady Astrid, or did she simply not know them? Noble children are sent away from their parents so young.*

'I seem cold to you,' said Rowena, 'though in truth I am not. I never knew my father.' She shrugged. 'I was his wage against his earthly sins, his payment to win him into heaven. Since infancy I have heard such things. If I am old for my age it is because my father wished me to be so.'

Listening, Magnus thought sadly that only briefly, in her delight of horses and in wishing to see her pony Apple, had Rowena shown her true age. *This little lass has been forced to grow up too soon.*

'Did you ever tell him you wished to be married when you were grown up?' Elfrida asked, her face and eyes warm with sympathy as she leaned toward the younger girl.

'He did not listen,' said Rowena.

No, the Giffords and Percivals do not trouble to hear. Magnus cleared his throat, uncertain what to say to that. Beside him, he heard Elfrida sigh.

'Truly, I will try to grieve as much as is fitting for my parents,' Rowena went on. 'But my family has never listened to me, or at least only Tancred has tried. Silvester — he too knows I am an heiress now, but he still does not want to wait until I am of age and marry me at a church door, or for us be married to each other by a priest. He says he does not trust priests.'

Given priests like Father Jerome, who can wonder? Yet, hearing the hurt in Rowena's voice, Magnus felt ashamed of his own male sex. *Silvester is a liar. He offers nothing real.*

'I cannot mourn much for my parents or brothers here, in Bittesby,' Rowena finished.

At that less-than-subtle reminder, Elfrida straightened and sighed a second time. 'I do sense we have little time,' she remarked, smoothing the gown over her knees and making sure her amulets and necklace were still secure. 'I do fear Silvester setting out in his wagon, taking one or more of the girls with him.'

Yes, there is that danger. 'But then I would catch him out on the road, without the townsfolk as his allies.'

'And if we miss his leaving? Or if one or more of the girls is harmed when you attack him?'

'I would harm none of them,' Magnus growled.

'No, but Silvester may, if he is desperate enough. We could try another way.' Elfrida belted the gown. 'I could creep into Silvester's and coax the girls out.'

'That would take too long,' said Rowena at once, swapping the broom from hand to hand. Unlike his wife, Rowena was not interested in his finer feelings, merely results. 'I like Magnus's plan better.'

Not my plan, or at least not a plan I feel easy with. These wretched females gang up on me. But then he rather liked the attention, the way Elfrida blew him a kiss, the way Rowena looked to him.

'I could come with you,' Rowena said.

Elfrida glanced at her. 'Can you run fast?'

The girl tugged at her ear and did not answer — clearly this was a sore point for her. Alfric rescued everyone by patting a stool and speaking for the first time in an age. 'Stay here with me, child. You are right pretty. That Silvester, he does not need any more young women.'

Elfrida leapt upon his surprising final statement. 'I thought Silvester was beloved in Bittesby.'

'Beloved, yes,' answered Alfric at once, head bowed as he worked on carving the bowl of the spoon. He spoke as if to convince himself. 'Silvester is beloved.'

Though not, it seems, by you. Magnus knew Alfric would admit to nothing more, that his confession had been a verbal slip. In the end what did it matter? The shelter that the old carpenter offered them all was enough.

Rowena meanwhile shrugged, muttered, 'Very well,' and asked Elfrida, 'Why fast? To avoid pursuit?'

'She thinks as you do, Magnus,' said Elfrida. 'Tactics.' She nodded to Rowena but Magnus caught the worry in her eyes.

She compares herself to creatures like Lady Astrid and thinks herself lacking because she was never trained to defend a castle, rocks and mortar. Can she not understand that is nothing? With her magic and healing she constantly defends living things. For all that she was, a witch and his wife, Elfrida undervalued herself, especially since the advent of Astrid and Tancred. It made him sorry. And he wanted to pitch the haughty pair into the nearest dung heap. *Let them look down their noses then.*

'You will stay here?' his anxious lass was asking Rowena, who huffed a little.

'A gentlewoman keeps her word,' she said stiffly.

Elfrida blushed and Rowena relented at once.

'Will you be long?' she asked, resuming her sweeping.

Not if I can help it, Magnus vowed to himself.

★ ★ ★

Elfrida borrowed a ewer from Alfric and walked out into Bittesby. She knew

Magnus was following her but such were the crowds now and his skill in tracking that she could not see him. She took a street running north of Silvester's house and doubled back, so people would not know which direction she had truly come from. Magnus, she sensed, was still with her, trusting her.

There is the well outside Silvester's. Entering Broad Street she moved toward it, noting that the purple and white shutters of her adversary's house were open. *Now, Silvester, see me. See me as Rowena. See me going away from your house.*

She remembered Rowena walking and copied the girl's fluid, tiny steps when she longed to stride. *See me going away, Silvester. Come out to find me.*

Behind her she heard the door being unlatched. She lengthened her steps, just a little, telling herself not to run. *Do not run yet, anyway . . .*

★ ★ ★

261

Magnus watched her dart past him along Broad Street, deftly threading between stalls and street sellers. *Never mind scaring the lasses out of doors,* he reminded himself sternly, *get Silvester when he comes outside to pursue Elfrida!*

But Silvester did not seem to be falling in with his change of plan. Elfrida had gone away, right along the street — Magnus spotted her in the jostling crowds, knowing her by the tilt of her head and her gracile, graceful figure. Meanwhile, the door to the fellow's house was open, hanging wide, but no one had emerged.

Where is he? There were no other doors. Magnus checked again for Elfrida, farther along the street. *Still safe. There she is, my clever witch-wife, still safe.*

He hesitated a moment longer, then charged straight at the door, straight for the house. *If the lasses inside think me a beast, so be it. I do not care if Silvester thinks me a monster. For him,*

I want to be a monster.

Fast as his thoughts, he raced, sprinting, gasping, yelling. He crashed through the open doorway, lurching into the house, and skidded to a stop on the floor tiles.

The place was empty. He roared through the rooms to make sure but found no one. The fire had been put out. The beds were made up. The crocks were washed.

In a tiny pantry he discovered a cellar. Racing down its steps he felt a strong through draft and saw a pale disc of light ahead, not from the way he had come in.

A passageway to the outside. Another way out. Silvester has taken his living trophies and escaped. He has been far cleverer than we realized.

Magnus ran down the passageway, emerging on another street altogether. Fresh cart tracks showed in a pile of horse dung, but Silvester was gone. *Did he see us with Rowena and decide to flee? Did the townsfolk warn him after all? And if they did, what else have they done for him?*

Liking matters less and less, Magnus started back for the carpenter's, running hard. As he ran, he stared at every face, watched every man, woman, and child he passed, listened intently below the commonplace clatter of carts and chorus of street cries for any unusual sounds, any false notes. *Elfrida and Rowena. I must make certain they are safe.*

★   ★   ★

Herbert the tailor turned the new bright coins in his hand and glanced along Broad Street. Easy money, he thought smugly, as he shifted left toward his stall. He might be married to one of Lord Silvester's cast-offs, but the lord always paid well and gave his Rametta new clothes each midsummer.

A massive fist clamped hard around his wrist. Off-balance, he punched back wildly but was spun like a top then battered into the dirt. Even as he tried to scream, a foot planted deep into his back, knocking the breath from him.

He writhed but the same huge fist locked about his throat, half-throttling him. As his sight blackened he saw his attacker looming over him, a big ugly brute, the same stranger whom he and Rametta had seen earlier that day. Worse, he heard him.

'One thing about bad spies, they always count their money too openly and they always come back to stare. Now, Master Tailor, you are going to tell me what you know and what you have told Silvester, and if I don't like it — '

Herbert choked, his mouth full of dust. Where was Rametta? Nowhere to be seen. 'Talk!' he wheezed. None of his neighbors were coming to help him, not against this man. If Rametta saw this monster, all she would do was scream. 'I'll talk!'

The stranglehold on his throat slackened and Herbert began to speak.

21

Elfrida knew she had been drugged, but she did not understand how. She had eaten and drunk nothing out on the streets. She had felt no one jostle or even brush against her. She had sensed nothing, no threat at all.

Except an instant before she lost consciousness there had been a strange trill of music issuing behind her. High as bird-song and as brief, it was so swift she wondered if she had imagined it.

Was that snatch of flute music a signal, perhaps, to one of the towns-folk?

Her back was sore, prickling. From a tiny arrow, perhaps, some kind of elf-dart?

Did a townsman shoot me in the back from an upper widow as I passed?

'Hush, or he will hear you. Silvester does not know you are awake yet,' whispered a girl, as Elfrida opened her eyes.

The dialect was close enough to that spoken around Norton Mayfield for Elfrida to understand. Careful not to move her head or body, she looked at the girl. 'I am Elfrida,' she said softly.

The girl looked unimpressed. 'You will not be Elfrida for long. My name is Rosalind now. I was baptized as Mary. Only Rowena and Ruth have kept their names. He likes names beginning with R.'

Silvester must have changed her name. 'Where are we?'

'Inside his house.'

'Is Silvester close?'

'In the next room, counting money.'

'Bribes to his former wives,' said another voice. 'One will be for capturing you. The instant Silvester learned about you from Herbert, he will have been keen you were caught. You are like us.'

Elfrida blinked and slowly sat up. She had been laid on a thin pallet on the floor, presumably by Silvester. Two pretty girls, small, thin, with red, chapped fingers and cool steady eyes watched her. As she had anticipated, they were dressed in gowns of purple and white. She swallowed and scowled.

'The dart leaves a foul taste,' said Rosalind. 'Get her some ale.'

'Get it yourself,' snapped the second girl. 'I am not your brother.'

Rosalind sighed and hauled herself off the floor to a sideboard, returning with cups and a jug of ale. She settled again on the floor with her legs straight out in front of her, poured three cups and pushed one toward Elfrida.

'My thanks.' Elfrida drank thirstily, assessing the room about her. They were in an upper chamber. The sun streamed in through half-open shutters. There were other pallets on the wooden floor, a sideboard by the door, and nothing else. 'Are the other girls with him?'

'What do you know?' demanded the second girl. 'Do you understand Silvester's pipes?'

I knew that snatch of pipe music was a signal of sorts! 'We have been searching for you, for all of you,' Elfrida said. She did not care if Silvester received this news. *Let him fear a little and sweat. Let him wonder who 'we' are.*

'Why?'

'To be sure you are safe. To return you to your families, should you wish it.'

Rosalind nodded. 'We are out of favor today. Silvester told us to stay with you, within the back room, instead of remaining with him.'

'You do not seem upset,' Elfrida remarked.

The second girl said, 'Ruth was the favorite until Silvester found Rowena and brought her to live with us. Now Ruth has vanished and so has Rowena. We are not keen to be favored.'

'Silvester is looking for Ruth and Rowena,' protested Rosalind.

'He *says* he is sending out his former wives to look,' shot back the second girl. 'Even now, with Rowena gone only this morning, he does not search himself.'

'Former wives?' prompted Elfrida. This was twice that the girls had mentioned them.

'When they become too old, or pregnant, Silvester sets them up here in Bittesby. They live as widows,' explained Rosalind. 'He takes care of us and them and his children. His former wives and bastards are respected in the town. No one troubles them, not even the priests.'

'I see.' Heart-sick at the idea that the priests of Bittesby colluded with Silvester, Elfrida found herself thankful that the appalling treatment of the girls was not, in fact, even more deadly. *Thank the Mother that Silvester had no worse fate in mind for them, as Magnus and I had feared. Thank the Holy Mother, too, that we did not go to a widow's house last night.* 'They do not re-marry?' Elfrida asked.

'Roxanne and Richmal have remarried,' said the second girl. 'He gave them a good dowry. Rametta married a tailor. She and Herbert live a few doors away. It was those two who likely spotted you and passed word about you to Silvester.'

Rosalind finished her ale and, leaving the cup, jumped to her feet. 'I should tell Silvester you are awake.'

She clattered out of the room. At once the second girl pointed to the pallet.

'Lie down again, pretend you are still groggy,' she ordered. 'Be quick! I do not have much time.'

Elfrida lay sideways on the lumpy pallet. 'What is your name?'

'Susannah, Susannah-Rose to Silvester, for I would not give up my name, but listen to me. I am becoming too old, do you understand? When we question him and lose our enchantment with him, Silvester does not like it. We become too old for him. And if we fall pregnant, he hates that. Mary, Rosalind as he calls her, is the same as me, beginning to doubt him, but she is more agreeable.'

'You sound beyond doubt.'

'I am. I cannot pretend for him anymore, but you should.' Susannah began to loosen Elfrida's hair, muttering, 'He likes unbound hair. Widen your eyes when he speaks, he likes that. Speak softly, blush if you can.'

'Please fasten my veil on the outside of the shutter,' begged Elfrida. *Magnus will be going wild, wondering where I am.* She would have done it herself but suspected that Susannah would be quicker and her own limbs still felt sluggish.

'Why? The window here looks down into nothing, believe me. We are lucky today to have the sun, usually we do not even have that.'

Elfrida crawled up the pallet to the wall and, inch by inch, hauled herself to her feet. When the world around her had stopped swaying a little, she tottered to the window.

'Watch out!' cried Susannah, gripping her shoulders as Elfrida felt herself toppling. She stared down, drawn by the drop, and felt despair, hot and sticky, rise in her throat.

This window did not look out over any street. When she glanced up, the sun shone over the roof tops but looking down took her into a different world. Here the houses were crowded cheek by jowl, with sagging, overlapping roofs and gutters. Taken as a whole these made a rough, enclosed circle about what had once been a yard. Down at the bottom of the circle there was a dim twilight of slime and dank, rotting refuse. As she peered deeper into the murk and caught the graveyard stench, Elfrida saw shapes rooting in the foul rubbish.

'Pigs sometimes break in,' said Susannah quietly. 'The dung wagon has not been here in years. People board up their lower windows and doors. No one goes in if they can help it.

'The pretty window, the good view, is out at the front,' Susannah continued. 'Where Silvester sleeps. We are not allowed there today.'

Would any signal be seen from here? *I have to try.* 'Please,' she said, holding out her veil, Rowena's veil.

Without further word or question, Susannah stepped lightly to the window and pinned the veil outside.

'How old are you Susannah?'

'Almost fifteen. I know you are older, too, but Silvester does not know yet.' She nodded to Elfrida's hands. 'I put your wedding ring onto your other hand after Silvester carried you inside and left you here. I do not think he has seen it. Men rarely notice details.'

'Thank you,' said Elfrida faintly, appalled at herself for not noticing the switch with the ring. She was rarely totally astonished, but Susannah was as self-possessed in her way as Rowena was in hers. *Is this girl a witch or healer? She is quick and sensible enough.* 'How did he catch you?' she asked.

'Not by any drugged dart!' Susannah snorted and flopped down on the pallet beside her. 'I am the eldest of seven, with six younger brothers. Silvester saw me washing my brothers' clothes in the stream, then fetching and carrying for them. He offered me more. It was good for the last two months, less good for the last two weeks.'

'Since Ruth and Rowena?'

Susannah threw her a scathing glance. 'I am not jealous, if that is what you think.' She shrugged her narrow shoulders. 'Silvester is another boy. I want a man. I want a man as a lover.'

'Are you all untouched?' Elfrida asked carefully.

'We are all virgins,' said Susannah bluntly. 'He says we shall be wed on midsummer's eve. The younger ones cannot wait, though how he will bed us all on one night I do not know.' She clicked her tongue. 'After midsummer, I doubt he will keep me long.'

'Will you come away with me?' Elfrida asked, whispering as she heard voices drawing closer.

'Need you ask?' Susannah rolled over

and began to pretend to snore.

Elfrida closed her eyes. She heard the door open and a tap, tap, tap of a cane. *Is Silvester lame, or does he walk with a stick for another reason?*

'Sleepy still,' said a male voice. 'Little sleepy head. Mistress Rebecca always tips her darts with a little too much poppy.'

'She was awake when I left her, Silvester. They were both awake,' protested Rosalind. 'I think Susannah-Rose sleeps too much.'

Rosalind might be in doubt of her tender feelings, but she was still seeking approval from Silvester, Elfrida thought. She felt a narrow stick prod gently at her stomach. She yawned and brushed at it as if she were still half-asleep.

'She is a redhead,' remarked a young girl, standing somewhere behind Silvester and Rosalind. 'Is that auburn, Silvester? Have I the word right?'

'She is as pretty as Ruth,' said another. 'Comely. Silvester, I think her gown looks like Rowena's. Yes, it does.'

'Prettier than Ruth and Rowena,' said

a third. 'Did I sleep for as long, Silvester?'

'Not half so pretty as you, my dears,' said Silvester now, chuckling when his adoring chorus giggled, 'but certainly as pretty as I was told this morning. I am right glad I whistled to Mistress Rebecca to watch out for her. Yes, Mistress Rebecca has done well, catching this maid after only one pipe signal. Ah, see, she wakes.'

Slim, dark, handsome, and with a winning smile — Silvester was all that. He looked young, but Elfrida sensed he was in his late twenties, like Magnus. He was not in purple and white, or at least not yet. Dressed in a rich, dark green tunic and a short, swirling cloak he wore his new clothes like a summer array. His three youngest girls surrounded him in a halo of nubile flesh, frowning when Elfrida widened her eyes and tried to look as appealing as possible. *How do I do it? Please, Holy Mother, let me gull him until I know more. He was told of me this morning.*

Was that when I returned to his house, or earlier? Has his network of spies learned where Rowena is, and told him? Does he know about Magnus?

Silvester was dangerous, certainly, because he seemed so kind, so ordinary, concerned with new clothes arid other trifles. But the knuckles that gripped the cane were hard and white and his eyes watchful.

'Sir? My ladies?' She was careful to include everyone and make her voice very low.

Silvester knelt by her pallet, leaning in. 'Do not be afraid,' he said gently. 'You are free of that bestial owner of yours.'

He means Magnus! So Silvester has seen him, or been told about him. Elfrida forced herself to remain still, apart from lowering her head so that he would not see the sudden anger in her face. His eyes, already no longer wary, followed her slight movement. Praying that she looked calm now, Elfrida locked her gaze with his and reached out carefully with her mind.

To her surprise, she sensed no magic in him at all.

This handsome monster is a contradiction. His clothes are new, this house is new but he clings to the old ways of worship. He seeks a kind of midsummer marriage to these girls, though I doubt he understands why such a marriage is sacred.

And why must all the girls have names beginning with R? Again she silently reached out and found Silvester's thoughts, his inward voice as high-pitched as a bat's.

'She looks like my old nurse Rosamund, and even more beautiful. I shall call her Rosamund.'

You loved Rosamund? Elfrida asked him with her mind.

'She was my nurse. She cared for me, healed me when I was sick and gave me flowers,' came back the light, tinkling answer.

In that instant, Elfrida glimpsed Silvester's former nurse. Dressed in white and purple, Rosamund had been a brown-haired, tiny, delicate young woman, one who followed the old ways. She had given Silvester his first hare's foot, his first posy of valerian and marigold and had danced with him at midsummer beneath an elder tree.

That is where Silvester got the idea for the wreath of valerian! Rosamund was a healer, almost a witch. She was like me . . . almost like me.

The realization startled Elfrida so much that she fell away from Silvester's mind and memories and returned in a rush to the present. Looking at him again, she saw the old ways honored in the hare's foot he had pinned to his bright cloak, in the sprig of rosemary he had tucked into his tunic. In spite of her earlier resolution, she felt a pang of pity for him.

Clearly sure of himself, of his charm, or charms, Silvester smiled at her. 'You are safe, little one. You do not need to be ashamed any more.'

His girlish chorus sighed, as if this were the most romantic speech they had ever heard. Elfrida felt a hopeful excitement. *Perhaps Silvester really does not know we are hunting him. Yes, of course he does not. He has taken young girls before and no one has stopped him. As Magnus and I suspected, he does have a help-mate, or help-mates, his former wives. Creatures like this Mistress Rebecca even do his hunting for him.*

Silvester brushed her gown. She forced herself not to react.

'Her gown is similar to Rowena's, but she wears a different belt to Rowena's, an old thing, far less elegant,' he remarked to the room at large. 'I gave Rowena a new belt.'

Elfrida half-expected the three younger girls to applaud these crashingly obvious observations — they looked desperate to applaud something. *He does not even recognize Rowena's gown, the gown he gave her. Of course, gowns and jewels are unimportant to him except as trinkets for his pets. He is rich enough for them to mean nothing.*

'You always buy us new clothes,' said

one of the girls now.

'And jewels,' said a second.

'I worship the Holy Mother in ancient ways, but I also like the new,' said Silvester.

'Like your walking stick!' said the third, beaming when Silvester gave her a little bow and twirled the cane.

Poor, deluded girls. So crazed for his approval . . .

Using his cane, Silvester lifted a tress of Elfrida's hair. 'Did your owner make you wear your hair loose? You may choose how you wear it with me.'

'I loosened her hair,' said Susannah, rolling back on the pallet to face Silvester.

For an instant Silvester's eyes and jaw hardened and the cane trembled in his fist. Crossed, he looked like Tancred and the Lady Astrid. *One of the Percivals for sure.* 'Susannah-Rose, you should not be doing that.'

The girl said nothing but her expression was stormy. 'Any word of Rowena or Ruth?' she demanded.

'Not yet, but then you know these things take time, Susannah-Rose.'

'Why did we have to rush out of the Broad Street house this morning?'

'I told you before, my dear, because of the rats. I need to return later and clear them.'

The kind of rat that walks on two legs and squeaks warnings. Elfrida consciously relaxed her tightened fists as she absorbed the news that they were not in the house in Broad Street, that Silvester was rich enough to have two, or even more houses, in Bittesby. *How will Magnus find me?* And hard on the heels of that thought, *After spotting Magnus this morning and hearing from his spies, Silvester decided that it was prudent to move. But still he feels no threat. He feels no true danger. He is so sure of his allies in this town.*

She was staggered by his arrogance, but the rest of his audience appeared convinced.

'Take care!' cried one of the younger girls.

Silvester smiled, his eyes shining like polished stones. 'Of course.'

'Where do you think Rowena and Ruth are?' persisted Susannah. 'Do you think they are safe?'

'My wives-to-be and former wives are always safe. I would know, otherwise.'

'How? How would you know?'

Silvester waved aside Susannah's question. Throughout their entire exchange he had spoken without concern for anyone, Elfrida noticed. *The girls he stole or beguiled away who are now lost to him. He does not really care where they are or what has happened to them. I was mistaken — to this man they are less than pets. To him, a tiny wreath of valerian is sufficient payment in exchange for kidnapping them from their families. Even Rowena, his own kindred, whom he took on orders and kept on a whim, means little or nothing to him. I do not need to pity him for the loss of his nurse. I doubt that he loved even her, not love as Magnus loves me.*

And I am most glad he does not

know how close Rowena is.

It was time to show these giddy girls how slight his 'caring' was. 'I feel sick,' she whispered, in the same tone Christina had used in the early stages of her pregnancy.

At once Silvester drew back and rose to his feet. 'Susannah-Rose, Rosalind, find her a bucket,' he said, all business. 'We shall be next door.' Quick as a kingfisher, he darted about and, with the cane, tapped the smallest girl on her polished, new shoes. ''Tis time for your lute lesson, Regina.'

Regina glowed and giggled as he took her hand in his, as he escorted her from the room. Following on, the two other girls trailed after the pretty pair like the streamers on a colorful cloak.

'See, Mary?' demanded Susannah, once the door was shut. 'He does not care if Ruth and Rowena are lost. 'Tis all novelty to him.'

'Maybe, maybe not.' Rosalind shook her head. 'But you should not make him angry.'

Elfrida rolled off the pallet and climbed to her feet, still drugged. Her vision danced for an instant and she feared to lose her breakfast but then she steadied. 'Ruth is back with her family,' she said quietly. 'So can you be, with your families. They love you still and do not change toward you.'

Go to the window, her intuition prompted, as the girls stared at her. Without questioning it, she slid her feet across the wooden floor. In truth she did feel queasy, light-headed, but what she had to say next was important, just as being by the window was vital.

She took a deep breath, hearing a faint creaking of the house timbers and the soft, plinking notes of a lute, hesitantly played. 'And Rowena is with us,' she added.

Susannah laughed and clicked her tongue, but Rosalind paled. 'So you say — ' she began.

A shadow fell across the room. 'My wife is right,' said Magnus, looming at the window.

Terrified of him tumbling into the filthy pit below them, Elfrida snatched for him. He gripped her hands strongly, saying, 'Nay, my lovely, never fret! I have climbed worse siege engines than this strong English wood. The rooftops here are easy and your veil a fine banner.'

He hooked himself through the open shutters, landing softly in a tiny patch of sunshine within the chamber, and smiled at the girls. 'Good morrow, damsels.'

His tunic has a new tear in it, Elfrida thought tenderly as she rapidly looked him over. *I will need to repair it.* Her heart lifted as his brown eyes lit again on her, warm as the summer sun. 'You are unharmed?' he asked.

Susannah slumped back onto a pallet in a faint. Rosalind gawped at his tall, muscular, scarred figure and burst into tears.

22

Elfrida was safe. At that moment Magnus cared for nothing else. She was pale and unsteady on her feet, but she was safe. To be sure, he took her hand in his.

'When I learned from the spy that you had been taken, that Silvester had signaled with his pipes that you should be taken, my world stopped,' he told her. *Now she is here and I am whole again.*

'A drugged dart got me,' she answered, with a faint smile. 'I felt no warning because the woman who shot me, Rebecca, did not intend to hurt me.'

'Even your magic cannot stop everything, elfling.'

She glanced at the girl weeping in the corner and said something in her own dialect. At once the girl sat down in the corner and rested her head on her arms. She looked calm enough to fall asleep.

'I must tend Susannah.' Slipping her hand from his, Elfrida crossed to the maid who had fainted. 'Is Rowena — ?'

'Still with our friend from this morning? She had better be.'

He wanted to open his arms and have Elfrida run to him but now, from deeper within this house, he heard new voices and footsteps. *Not hurrying, because Silvester does not know he has been found. None of his spies think to watch the rooftops.*

Which in itself made a kind of sense. Magnus himself had almost missed the fluttering veil, swinging in that dark well. Its movement had alerted him as, intent on the spy's confession, he scrambled from roof to roof, climbing almost as fast and nimbly as he had done as a boy. There had been one nasty instant when he had to shin down to the window and hang one-handed over the black, stinking, closed-in yard, but that was over. *I do not need to do it again, that is for sure.*

Savoring that thought, not hurrying, Magnus turned to face his enemy.

The man was a surprise in only one thing — his height. *He is even taller than me.* For the rest, Silvester was exactly as Magnus had imagined, a slim, handsome, dapper adversary, strolling arm in arm with three pretty girls. The girls screamed the instant they clapped eyes on Magnus, who shut out their dreadful caterwauling and called out, 'Give them up and go free.'

'No!' screamed the girls.

'No!' cried Elfrida.

Silvester — who else would it be, as haughty as a cat and with a young maid hung on each arm? — flung back his head to glower down his nose. 'How came you?'

Magnus was already weary of the fellow. 'Step away, Silvester,' he warned. 'My quarrel is with you. Release them.'

'No!' shouted the girls a second time. One even stepped in front of her captor, spreading her arms wide to defend him. Over her tiny head and fluttering hands, Silvester met his eyes and smirked.

Arrogant Percival bastard. 'Hiding behind girls, are we?'

Silvester widened his smile and continued to let the girl stand between them. 'You are not welcome here, knightling. Are you from my foolish cousins? They will not have Rowena.'

'Prove it,' said Magnus. 'Fight me.' *Knightling, eh? We shall see.*

Silvester shrugged. 'How does that prove anything?'

'That you care enough?' said Magnus, amazed by what the fellow had already done and said, or rather not done.

'Here!' cried Elfrida suddenly. Leaving the girl she called Susannah, she scrambled over pallets to join him. As she came, she flung up a hand, showing her wedding ring. 'Here is proof of caring, of true love! This ring is a public sign of our love! Magnus is my husband! My real husband. We were married by a priest, at the door of the church!'

Silvester glanced at her, not in the least disconcerted it seemed by this new information. 'So he is yours and these are mine,' he said, utterly shameless. 'We marry at the midsummer.'

'For how long?' demanded Elfrida.

Magnus sensed a movement from the girl sitting down in the corner. He glanced at her and she flinched but then she stared at Elfrida's raised hand, at the bright ring of gold on her finger.

'When Regina and the others are as old and wise as Susannah, will you be tired of them as well?' Elfrida went on.

The smallest of the younger girls, possibly Regina, began to bite her fingernails.

Do not draw your sword. Elfrida's silent warning sounded like a bell in Magnus's head. He scowled, but only because his wife had no need to tell him his business. *As if I would in this cramped little room, with these fretful lasses.*

He tapped his sword belt instead.

Moving with graceful slowness, Silvester put aside the cane he had been carrying and rested it against a wall. 'I do not have to fight you,' he said.

'No, he is a beast!' whimpered another girl. 'He will never fight fair.'

She is young. She thinks she loves Silvester. Despite his brave thoughts, Magnus died a little inside. He looked across to Elfrida, the one who knew him, who loved him.

Silvester moved then, but he did not charge. He grabbed a girl, yanked her back against him, put a knife to her throat.

'Easy, easy there.' Magnus lowered his hands. Around him the room seemed brighter as he focused in on that sharp blade, the twitching, white-faced child, Silvester's cold eyes.

'Holy Mother,' breathed Elfrida. 'This is no marriage. Silvester, please. Let her go. She never hurt you. She is like Rosamund, your nurse. None of your girls, your wives, have hurt you. They have done you nothing but good. Is this how you repay your maidens?'

Magnus watched the glitter of the blade, stared into Silvester's face. 'Only one right way to end this,' he said quietly. 'You know. You know.'

'The townsfolk love me,' said Silvester, blinking wildly.

'Aye, maybe they do for now,' Magnus agreed. 'But they are out there. I am here.'

'As am I.' Elfrida snapped her fingers and the scent of valerian filled the room. 'The wisdom that your nurse Rosamund told you, I know it too. And I know more.'

Silvester looked at her. What he saw in her slight, contained figure, in her warm eyes and implacable mouth, Magnus could not guess, but the air between them shimmered. The scent of valerian grew stronger. Still he watched the knife. *Let Elfrida work her way and I will work mine.*

The glitter flashed and Magnus lunged, catching the girl, wrapping his arms tight about her, ignoring her screams, turning so she would not see.

Silvester ran toward the open window, lashing out as Elfrida tried to stop him, leapt through it and fell into the darkness without a sound.

Crossing the silent room, Magnus looked out. He knew no one could survive such a drop but he wanted to be sure. Peering down into the gloom he spotted Silvester far below. He lay sprawled and broken, on his back, his head twisted to an impossible angle. The pigs rooting in the muck were already showing interest and closing in.

Magnus crossed himself. 'Silvester is dead.' What else could he say? There was no way to soften it. Gently he closed the shutters.

★ ★ ★

Shocked beyond screaming or tears, the girls followed Elfrida's rapid prompts now without protest. Gather their things. Follow her down the stairs. Wait with her while Magnus looked out.

The wagon Silvester used was outside the house — no luck was involved, merely there was no space else to leave it but the street. Magnus wanted to drag the pallets into it, but Elfrida knew they had to make haste. She shepherded Susannah and the others into the wagon and closed its covers.

'I will fetch Rowena and our horses,' Magnus said, and he went off, striding away in the hazy sunlight.

Elfrida waited inside the wagon, her mind buzzing like a hive of bees. Silvester had no real magic, but that final clash of wills between them, where he had drawn on his memories of the old wisdom, that had surprised and drained her.

Though it is still before noon I could lie down and sleep.

But of course that was impossible. She, Magnus, even the girls, they were all in danger. Before tottering outside into the street and drawing out the girls she had cast a hiding spell, but still she was not certain whether their hasty leaving had been spotted by one of Silvester's spies. She did not know for how long the girls' shock would keep them quiet. She did not know if the girls would ever forgive her or Magnus, whether they would always blame them for Silvester's death. She did not know how to drive the wagon.

I must learn quickly, though, for Magnus cannot do it. I may gull the town gateman and convince him I am driving Silvester, but Magnus is too conspicuous. He will need to stay inside the wagon and ensure our passengers keep silent.

It shamed her that she would soon be using her husband's looks against him, casting him as a threat, but she and Magnus had no choice. *To escape Bittesby we must do this.*

* * *

The day passed sluggishly for Magnus. Jammed in the wagon with his knees under his chin and the girls crouched as far away from him as they could manage was torture. With Rowena driving the wagon and Elfrida riding beside her, they edged through the streets at the tedious pace of a goose drover.

Jolted about inside the wagon, Magnus hated the way the girls would not look at him. He longed to comfort them, but they whispered among themselves. He dreaded one of them asking again if Silvester was dead, or asking how the man looked in death. He wished they were less pale, less stricken. Since Silvester had dived from the window they seemed incapable of reacting. Rowena, restored to them, smiling, greeting each by name, offering them a bowl of strawberries she had been given by Alfric, was met with mute disinterest.

'We must give them time,' Elfrida had whispered to him before she joined Rowena at the front of the wagon. 'They do not know who they are anymore.'

How much time? Magnus thought. How much longer?

And the wagon inched on.

* ★ ★

Not until they had passed out through the town gate and were grinding along the road did Elfrida dare to relax. Magnus changed places with Rowena then and they could speak together as he drove.

'We can go no faster than this,' he said. 'Our horses are unused to pulling a wagon.'

Elfrida glanced behind, at Bittesby's slowly disappearing roofs and church spires. 'It cannot be helped.' She, too, longed to go faster. 'I am glad the gate keeper did not notice the horses.'

'Too busy staring at Rowena?'

'Yes.' Elfrida watched the passing countryside for a moment. 'Did you know she has brought ale and food with her?' she asked then. 'Alfric was most generous.'

'Humph! I know there is a story with Alfric. We may never know it, but he did not like Silvester, did he?'

Elfrida crossed herself, trying not to

think of the dark, fetid yard. 'What now?'

Magnus lightly snapped the reins. 'We go home.'

Home, where Tancred was waiting and Peter and the Templars would have gathered. 'What do we tell them about Silvester?'

'As little as possible, until the lasses are settled again.'

Home, where Tancred will waste no time in telling Rowena I am a peasant. And how will Magnus and I be with each other? What did he mean when he compared me to Christina and said later that he should be more of a man? Did he mean what I think he meant, that he wants a child with me? Why should that be a difficulty? I wish I knew more but he keeps his thoughts guarded and I cannot sense them.

Elfrida sighed. *I wish I knew more.*

23

The journey took two days, but they had no other trouble. No mob from Bittesby roared out after them, which told Magnus that the townsfolk had really believed Silvester was riding with them in the back of the wagon. *He must have done so on his travels before, a piece of luck for us.*

Taking their ease, they moved slowly through the landscape. At close to sunset on the second day, calling to encourage his flagging horses, Magnus brought the wagon into Norton Mayfield. The May pole he had ordered was already set up in the church meadow. Its ribbons and streamers hung limply in the baking evening heat, fluttering in only the strongest of summer breezes.

Excellent. We shall have some dancing later. Why not? Is today not a celebration? Elfrida and I have won! We have

301

the lasses back, all of them, and safe.

He knew that he and Elfrida were still not fully at ease with each other, but that would surely come. *It must. God would not be so unkind as to leave us this way.*

I must court her again. The decision pleased him and he winked at his wife, perched nervously on the wagon beside him. When she blushed like a young lass, he laughed aloud, delighted with the omen.

To add to his sense of well-being and victory, soldiers unknown to him but wearing the badges of Peter came out of village houses and saluted as he passed. Ahead, he could see Mark posting sentries and ordering the lighting of the fire in the great hall. The doors to his manor stood open, as they always did when he was home in the summer.

Peter of the Mount, golden-haired, blue-eyed, bright and deadly as a dragon, sprinted out of the manor house way in front of the shorter-legged Tancred.

'Hellbane!' Magnus bawled to him,

glad to see his friend.

'Magnus!' Peter clapped him hard on the shoulder and whirled Elfrida off the wagon seat. 'Look at you, more beautiful than ever!'

'Hey, I am a married man.'

'Not you, fool! Your wife! My Alice sends her best love . . . '

Throughout Peter's enthusiastic greetings, Magnus was aware of the wary silence in the wagon behind him, the polite and careful silence in the hall ahead of him and of Tancred, pounding past the foam-flecked horses. Quick as a whip, he leaned down from the wagon and hauled the lad onto the seat beside him.

'Steady,' he warned in a steely voice, when Tancred drew breath to protest.

Squirming in his grip, Tancred was already red-faced. 'I want to see Rowena! You have no right to keep her from me!'

So the lad had heard the rumors and probably knew the news from Baldwin, who had ridden out to escort the wagon to the manor.

Magnus put his face so close to Tancred's that he could see the wispy down on the boy's face. He spoke very distinctly, keeping tight rein on his temper. 'Does Rowena want to see you? Not yet, I suspect, not after a long journey. Do you want her to be less than her best? Or you less than yours?'

Calculation replaced greed on Tancred's ruddy face. He nodded, said stiffly, 'You are right, Magnus. My thanks,' then looked uncertain what to do next.

Magnus took pity on him. 'Why not see if the bath-house is ready for Rowena?' He did not mention the other girls. Sadly, he knew that to speak of them and their trials would cut no ice at all with Tancred.

The boy's lower lip curled. 'The Templars are in there. Again!'

Magnus let the chuckle out, recalling the Templars' love of bathing in Outremer. 'Then go in and request their departure. Tell them ladies wish to bathe.'

Tancred hurtled off like a comet and Magnus scratched at the cloth door of the wagon. He did not put his head through, lest the maids cry at him again.

'You shall soon be able to bathe and change, my . . . ' His voice faded. What could he call them? 'My guests,' he finished weakly.

'Thank you,' called Rowena from within, serene as a floating swan.

Magnus flinched as Susannah's head appeared above his through the cloth door. The girl, who had fainted when she first saw him, now tugged on his tunic.

'Is your squire Baldwin for the feast tonight?'

I did not know there was going to be a feast, but why not? He nodded.

'Will he help me down from the wagon now? And will your friend Sir Peter help the others?'

Magnus glanced at Peter, still whispering in his wife's ear. Elfrida was nodding, which meant she and Peter were plotting. He glanced at Susannah and found her looking at him quite steadily. She gave a tiny shrug, almost of apology.

Of course, Peter is handsome, like Silvester.

'Your wish is my command.' Tasting the bitterness of his own mangled looks afresh, Magnus put his fingers in his mouth and whistled hard for his squires.

★ ★ ★

Elfrida was as busy as she had ever been. At harvest time in Top Yarr, her old village, she had been busy. In winter, healing the elderly and sickly, she had been busy. A house filled with bawling knights she did not know and nervous, prone-to-weeping girls was a different challenge, but she was busy again.

Finding gowns for the girls was her hardest problem. While they were in the bath house, Elfrida hurried to her bed-chamber and pulled her clothes onto the bed. A quick count told her she had four, plus the brown 'gown' she had been given as an insult in Lord Richard's manor.

I need one more gown from somewhere. More than one, for two of these need washing.

She sighed, thinking of the ever-present lack of a laundress at the manor.

Wait, did the Lady Astrid collect all her luggage?

It was no surprise to Elfrida that the lady had left a clothes chest behind. Opening it, she had just put her hands inside when Magnus, followed by Peter, strode into their solar-bedroom. Glimpsing their faces, she knew this meeting was meant to be private.

'Magnus.' She began to rise off her knees.

'Any trouble here?' he was asking Peter.

Magnus had not heard her. She found herself crouching down again, unsure whether to interrupt more loudly.

'Only the Templars taking up permanent residence in your bath house.'

Peter, also unaware that she was in the chamber, scratched his groin. 'How are you, man?'

'All the better for being home.'

'Which one of those gigglers that you brought with you is Rowena Gifford?'

'The prettiest, and she does not giggle at all. You are not going to carry on your quarrel with her, are you, Peter?'

'Grant me more sense and honor than that! Will I meet her soon?'

'Soon as you like.'

'Your Elfrida is looking too pale.'

'I know.' Magnus stretched his arms above his head before punching Peter playfully on a shoulder. 'That bitch Astrid has unsettled her.'

'So settle her again. Let the youngsters marry or be re-betrothed, have your saint's day, sort out the Percivals and Giffords and get Elfrida pregnant. You want an heir, do you not?'

'I need an heir. That is why I — '

Magnus suddenly spotted her. Perhaps she had started, or made a sound.

His eyes widened and she was sure he was blushing beneath his beard.

'Excuse me.' Mortified herself, fearful, too, that he might think she was spying on him, Elfrida picked up her skirts and hurried away, leaving the chest open. Pretending not to hear his call — 'Elfrida, please wait!' — she ran into the great hall and then farther out, rushing into the garden.

That is why I married her. That was what he had been going to say. What else? *He has married me for an heir. That is what knights and nobles do.*

Hiding herself behind a heavily laden plum tree, she let the tears come. *I thought we had married for love . . .*

★ ★ ★

Magnus started after his wife but Peter stopped him. 'What ails her?'

Magnus stared at Peter's hand and his friend released his arm as if he had been scorched. He shook his head, disliking Elfrida overhearing anything.

309

He had been speaking to Peter man-to-man, of heirs because that is what men expected to hear. But he should not have started to mention the Arab learning — that was the kind of confession Tancred might have made, not him.

At least I did not say it. But what had Elfrida been expecting him to admit?

Uneasy, he bade a crisp farewell to his friend and went in search of her.

★ ★ ★

He tracked her down in the garden. Kneeling on the path, she was examining an obvious weed as if it was a mandrake but had not removed it.

'Elfrida.'

She looked up at him, love and hurt shining in her eyes.

'I am sorry,' he said helplessly, ashamed of being caught gossiping with Peter. *Had I not spotted her I might have even spoken of my book itself, as well as the eastern learning. What is wrong with me? Am I an ale-wife to chatter so?* 'Whatever I have done, or not done, I am sorry for it.'

'Never fret, Magnus.' She made a good attempt at the words but her heart was plainly not in them and she gave no explanation for her swift departure. Possibly not seeing his outstretched hand, she rose to her feet. 'I must get on. The girls need new robes, clean ones at least, and I cannot think where to find any. I hoped Lady Astrid might have left behind some clothes, but it is all shoes.'

'Do not go.' He did not mean it as an order, though it sounded one.

She smiled at him and now she took his hand and gently squeezed his fingers. 'I am not leaving you. Just give me time, Magnus, a little time, yes?'

She stood on tiptoe and kissed him. 'I love you.'

'And I — '

'I must return to my duties.'

She slipped by him, not leaving, returning to her duties. *What does she mean? What little time? Surely it cannot be our different stations in life again? What must I do to prove I love her?* Determined to thrash it out once and for all, Magnus started after her.

He was within two paces of her when a trumpet call had him turning toward the road beyond the manor. Elfrida spun round, too, and moaned when she realized who was coming.

'Holy Mother, as if there is not already enough to deal with!'

Magnus came behind her and clasped her shoulder, glad to feel that this burn of anger was not directed at him. 'We shall manage. Do not let her trouble you, my lovely. We shall do well.' *Better this, far better, than a troop of knights and men at arms.*

It was the Lady Astrid.

24

Riding in on a pure white palfrey, Lady Astrid was clearly intent on making an impression. She wore a golden gown, with long sweeping sleeves that trailed on the ground. Her maids were garbed in scarlet and cream, and her herald the same.

'No guards with her,' remarked Magnus. 'Has she come with kinsman's Richard's blessing or not, I wonder? Is there a troop hiding or waiting behind, on the road?'

'She knows she need not fear you,' Elfrida replied, wishing she had not heard him earlier, talking to Peter. *People who listen in never learn good of themselves.* And did it matter? Magnus loved her in his way and of course he required an heir, what man did not? 'I wish she were not here.'

'True for me also, my heart, but we

313

must be fine hosts.'

'For the girls, also?'

Magnus gave her a steady look. 'For them, too,' he said drily. 'Now, you go the bath-house and ensure the girls are content and I will speak to the Templars. Then I shall greet the lady. Splendor in Christendom! I cannot wait to watch her face curdle when Tancred tells her that Rowena is found.'

'Look at her gown!' Elfrida knew she was lamenting over trifles but could not stop herself. Even after travel and dusty roads, Lady Astrid glittered like a new coin. *She is in gold and I cannot even clothe six girls.*

Magnus hooked her off her feet, gave her a hard kiss and set her down, facing the bath-house. 'I am on that,' he said cryptically, and strode off.

Elfrida sped to the bath-house. Before she opened the door, she heard giggles issuing from inside. Dare she hope that the youngsters were starting to look forward to being reunited with their families, rather than looking backward to their time spent with Silvester?

On the slow journey to Norton Mayfield the girls had spoken over and over about Silvester. Elfrida feared they were trying to convince themselves that he was still alive, although no one could have survived that fall into the dark yard and Magnus himself had told them Silvester was dead. For the first day and night only Susannah and Rowena had eaten anything and none of the girls, apart from Rowena, would look directly at Magnus.

That is slowly changing. Susannah speaks to him now. If I could only speak as easily . . . 'I do not doubt his love so why do I fear his tiring of me later?' she said aloud, pushing open the door. *Why should I dread that Magnus may be like Silvester in this regard? Silvester is dead! The girls are safe. Stop this whimpering over your differences in rank! You were never troubled before. You are a witch! You have status. And if it does not matter to him it should not matter to you.*

Pausing by the door, she waited until she could see through the steam. Rowena, settled naked on the warm bath-house stones, waved to her. Susannah, rarely abashed, called out, 'Will you help me wash my hair?'

The other girls, Rosalind, Regina, Richenda and Richildis, whispered behind their hands. They had each taken a cup of ale and some berries, Elfrida noticed. *Their appetite and interest returns, which is good.* While they were traveling in the wagon, she had sung over them each night, a tiny charm to settle them and ensure they slept without dreams. *We should be telling their families.*

But not quite yet, she sensed. She wanted their homecomings to be smooth, without regret. She did not want them hankering after Silvester, or they would not settle.

And Magnus understood this. Without her explaining anything, he had already asked, while they and the wagon had plodded past the church at Norton Mayfield, 'The girls are to sleep in our solar-bedroom tonight?'

Elfrida nodded, recalling the memory, and picked up a pail to help Susannah. She had wet Susannah's dark hair thoroughly when a brisk knock on the door told her Magnus was outside.

'Towels and gowns!' he called out. 'In a basket on the threshold. When you are ready, Peter, Tancred, Baldwin, and I will escort you.'

'Thank you!' answered Elfrida, happy to see excitement on the girls' faces. From such things came small, everyday progress. *Gowns, too, and where has Magnus found those?* She heard him striding off, so could not ask. *When will Magnus and I be truly easy with each other again?*

'We choose our escorts, do we not?' Susannah suddenly demanded through a wall of wet hair.

'We do,' Rowena replied, running a comb through Regina's blond curls. 'I am for Magnus, if you do not object, my lady.'

Still thinking of herself and Magnus

and those mystery gowns, Elfrida started and shook her head. 'He has two arms and will gladly squire us both.' *Unless he escorts Lady Astrid? No! Stop this folly! Magnus deserves your love and your pride! Be a witch, be a lady, be Elfrida!*

'My thought exactly,' said Rowena.

'Not Tancred?' Elfrida asked, pouring rosemary-steeped warm water through Susannah's hair. She caught the whispered, 'Peter!' from the younger girls and smiled, a little sadly. Of course the young ones would be beguiled by the outward show of Peter's fair good looks. *And Peter is no Silvester.* But Rowena was answering and she should pay attention.

'Tancred may wait to escort me.'

'You have not forgiven him yet?' asked Susannah, peering through her dripping fringe. 'For not riding to your rescue?'

'I wish to honor Magnus, who did,' said Rowena blandly.

Elfrida bit her lip to stop the chuckle

escaping. Rowena was right — she only hoped the lesson would do Tancred good. 'Your kinswoman, the Lady Astrid, is also here,' she added, unsure if this news was a warning or a joy.

'I shall be pleased to make her reacquaintance,' Rowena replied, still very bland. 'And that of her Father Jerome, of course.'

The way she spoke suggested to Elfrida that Rowena knew very well that Astrid and the priest were lovers. *Though how will the lady and the priest deal with each other now, I wonder?* 'I will bring in the towels and gowns.'

Determined to be as calm and gracious as Rowena, and with all her guests in the great hall, Elfrida wove past the bath tubs to the doorway.

* * *

The Templars had done them proud, was Magnus's first thought, when Elfrida and the rest of the womenfolk — he could not call these sweeping damsels girls — glided from the bath-house. He had asked, for the sake of old fellowship in Outremer, and the knights had responded for the same reason, piling him up with every scrap of silk in their luggage.

And Elfrida, his clever witch-wife, had known what to do with it.

'Magnus.' She smiled at him now and he basked in her approval.

'My lord?' Rowena, clad in a rustling sky-blue silk sheath, ignored the pop-eyed Tancred and approached. 'Will you do me the honor of escorting me with your lady wife?' Rowena smiled very sweetly but raised her voice so the hovering Tancred heard every word. 'I can never thank you enough for your rescue.'

Tancred looked ready to spit nails. Magnus bowed and offered his left arm to Rowena and his right to Elfrida. Farther off in the yard, Susannah was already arm in arm with Baldwin, who looked as if a sling-shot stone had hit him. The lass was in silver and yellow and moved like an empress, so Magnus was not surprised by his squire's dazed reaction. Piers, his other squire, looked equally dazzled in the company of Rosalind, who was now Mary again.

Arm in arm with Richildis and Richenda, both pretty and animated in their clouds of pink and white silks, Peter winked at him. He had taken the measure of Lady Astrid in the hall, describing her to Magnus as 'haughtier than the devil.' Now he called out, 'You are right,' and nodded to Rowena, adding in their private, crusader argot, 'one Gifford I can admire.' Clearly Peter was enjoying himself and ready to enjoy more.

'Sir?' Regina, the smallest and youngest of those rescued from Silvester's house, now held out a work-roughened hand to the glowering Tancred. 'Will you guide me?'

The boy blushed, perhaps finally recognizing this tiny peasant maid in her pale green gown as a fellow Christian soul. Without further prompting, he took her slim little fingers, gently tucking them through his arm. As they all began to proceed across the yard, Magnus heard Regina say, very softly to Tancred, 'My name is Regina, or Bertha. My family call me Bertha.'

'I like Bertha,' said Tancred quietly, rejecting the name Silvester had given her.

Magnus smiled as Rowena squeezed his fingers and Elfrida gripped his arm. 'Little steps,' he heard his wife say, and then they were climbing the stairs to the hall.

'Sir Magnus!' cried Lady Astrid, the instant he crossed the threshold, bursting into a flurry of Norman French, 'For shame, where is Rowena? And where is your wife? Why is she not here to welcome me?'

Magnus looked coolly at the golden figure seated at the high table, quite unmoved by her outburst. Father Jerome, poor fool, had actually changed seats with one of the Templars to sit beside her, but the lady took no heed of him. Now though, the priest rose, the name 'Rowena' forming on his lips. Lady Astrid, despite her complaint, seemed not to have noticed her ward.

Tancred, kicking aside a stool so his companion would not be impeded, stepped forward. 'Good evening, aunt,' he said in English. 'May I present — ?'

'Be quiet, Tancred,' snapped the lady in the same tongue, not so gracious.

She really is insufferable, Magnus thought.

'I have found that the Lady Astrid rarely listens,' said Rowena, pitching her voice perfectly to fill the hall, 'But she and the Lady Elfrida, my friends, and you worthy knights and companions, you shall hear me now.'

Two spots of red color appeared on the Lady Astrid's cheeks, making her appear like an angry doll, Magnus decided. She swallowed whatever retort she was about to make and drummed her fingers on the table. *Very wise, my lady. Things are moving way beyond your control.*

To his surprise and delight, Rowena

turned and embraced him and then she hurried to embrace Elfrida. After hugging his wife tightly, she again faced the high table.

'We, these other maidens and myself, we were all stolen away by Silvester Percival. No one troubled to look for us.'

'Not so!' muttered Tancred, 'And I brought you Apple!' but Rowena quelled him with a glance.

'Not for all of us,' she continued. 'Only my lord Magnus and my lady Elfrida took the pains and care to discover our whereabouts, and to bring us all safely away. Now we are returned and things are no longer as they were.'

Rowena smiled, but her blue eyes narrowed. 'I am not the little girl who embroidered daisy chains on her head-rail and who wished to please everyone. I was obedient to my family and they left me with Silvester. Since then I have grown up.'

'Rowena?' said Tancred, hesitation and fear showing nakedly in his square, fair face. *Finally the young thick-head realizes he could lose her.*

She smiled at him, then with her lips and her eyes, where Magnus would have made the lad sweat a while longer. 'For this reason,' she went on, 'I wish to re-plight my troth to Tancred, before this noble company and household. I wish to do so particularly before Magnus and Elfrida, who have fast become my mentors and guides as to how a lord and lady should be.'

Father Jerome gave a half-cry, hastily stifled, and Magnus sensed his own priest looking at him. He nodded to Father Luke and then to Elfrida. Never a dull man, the priest raised a hand to Elfrida, who glanced at Magnus, grinned at Father Luke and mouthed, 'Yes.'

Father Luke smiled and called for silence. 'I am honored to witness this betrothal in the name of the church. Tonight or tomorrow, if you wish it.'

'I accept,' said Rowena, seizing her own destiny with a smoothness Magnus could only admire. 'Tomorrow, with you and Father Jerome and my Lady Astrid in attendance.'

Very neat. She ensures they have to support her and has witnesses to prove it. Now, whatever Lady Astrid might have wanted or plotted, why ever she came here, she is committed to Rowena and Tancred. Lord Richard will not be pleased, but Lord Richard is doubtless still at Castle Rocher Noir, seeking a Percival who will never be found. And Richard and Astrid must have had a falling out. I cannot say I am surprised.

The thoughts ran like quicksilver through his mind, then people reacted. Peter cheered and danced with his two ladies, cutting a caper with them on the herb-strewn floor. Elfrida laughed, her color making her brighter than the fire. Tancred stared at his bride and only moved toward her when Bertha gave him a kiss. The rest of the hall erupted.

Through the giddy haze of stamping, yelling well-wishers, Magnus spotted the Lady Astrid and Father Jerome, both frozen in their seats. Despite her golden gown and her well-dressed hair, her maids in attendance, Lady Astrid looked defeated. She looked old.

Were I more a Christian, I would pity you, lady, but I am not and I do not.

He beckoned to the servers. 'More ale and food for everyone!' *If we are short of both tomorrow, so be it. These young folk, all of them, deserve a celebration today.*

Elfrida leaned into him and against him. 'Peter has brought much provender with him, wine and bread and cheese, too, and more. Dates and figs . . . '

That was what she and Peter had been plotting!

'Excellent!' He kissed her heartily to show Tancred how to do it, then tenderly, for him and Elfrida. 'I will want a dance from you later,' he warned his wife.

'So long as you do not mind me stumbling the steps.'

'Never.' He stroked her cheek. 'Never, my heart.'

'Thank you again for the silks.' Elfrida

stroked her gown of dark blue silk as if it was a cat. She looked beautiful in it, he thought, but more beautiful out of it.

He hugged her tightly, realizing in that instant that her gown was scarcely stitched together, merely held by pins and brooches. *Of course she would not have had time for anything else.* He pictured unpinning her later and smiled. 'The Templars owe me. They were happy to help.'

'None of us used the purple silk.'

Which was significant, Magnus guessed, but he kept his voice easy. 'So the knights can have that back.'

'If they wish . . . Oh, did I tell you? Susannah wants to stay. She will be our laundress.' Elfrida chuckled. 'She says she has washed things for years without payment, so is happy to do so for gold. She says her kindred will be happy with gold as well.'

Magnus grinned at Susannah's bargaining. The lass would go far, he reckoned. 'Baldwin will be pleased.'

'Of that I am certain. And Rowena

says she will allow Tancred to escort her to see Apple later on.'

'Not too late, I hope.'

'Rowena knows what she is doing. She has already accepted Githa back again as her maid.'

Magnus grinned a second time. Here was another lass who would go far. 'I am relieved she is still young enough to like her pony.'

'So am I.' Elfrida shook her head. 'She is eleven, Magnus! What will she be at twelve? What will she be when she comes of age and marries in truth?'

They stood together, watching Rowena, Tancred and the others, Magnus breathing in his wife's delicious perfume and anticipating the night.

25

The dancing went on until moonrise and beyond, moving out of the hall to the newly erected May pole. *Can it be a May pole when it is almost midsummer?* Elfrida wondered. Leaving Magnus talking of Outremer with Peter and the Templar knights, she hurried away from the church yard to the manor.

Passing the garden, she saw a tall, lonely figure, wandering alone, without her usual hovering priest. Lady Astrid had declined to take part in the dancing, but she could not retire. Tonight the solar-bedroom belonged to the girls. Wanting everything to be fine and dainty for Rowena, Susannah, and the others, Elfrida slipped into the chamber.

Magnus had been in before her. His small clothes chest had been shifted from the back wall to the head of the bed, but was not back in its usual place.

There was a deep alcove in the wall where the chest normally stood, a secret place where her husband kept his treasures.

He had taken the relic, she understood, knowing he had secreted it there when Lord Richard's herald had reluctantly handed it over. Was he going to give it to Tancred and Rowena and let them deal with Tancred's older brother? It made sense. Elfrida pulled the chest to drag it across the secret alcove again.

There in the alcove was Magnus's book, his bestiary. Elfrida paused and drew it out, opening it on the bed. Magnus was proud of his book and rightly so, for it was a beautiful thing, well made, full of illustrations and learning. She slowly turned the pages, smiling when she saw the porcupine again, remembering the first time he had spoken of the beast.

He is learned and kind, as handsome within as Peter is on the outside. Even the youngest girls were starting to recognize that. Regina, who now called herself Bertha again, had danced with him.

We must send word to their families tomorrow; let them know their missing girls are safe.

For tonight, that would keep. She turned a few more pages. And stopped. There, in a detailed series of illuminations, was part of a thesis of Arab learning, dealing with female fertility and pregnancy. Slowly, she made out the text, studying each picture in turn.

The book claimed that to get a woman with child, a man should mate with her 'in the manner of a stallion and a mare,' for five times in succession.

Magnus wants me to have a baby.

Their recent lovemaking confirmed it. He had taken the advice of this book to heart and acted upon it.

Elfrida closed the book and put it back in the alcove, pushing the chest in front of the hiding place. She crouched, resting her head on the bed. *We shared so many nights of pleasure. Was it only for a child?*

She remembered his strange mood before they had traveled to Bittesby, his bitter, mysterious words, 'So small you are. So slender still.' And then his accusation, 'If I were only more a man, this caper of yours would be impossible.' She considered his war wounds, his grief each time maids were terrified of his looks. The fragments came together in a rush and she understood.

Magnus fears I might leave him. He wishes me to have a child not only to have an heir but to bind us beyond all breaking.

For an instant it stunned her and she was angry he would think that, but then was she not the same in a different way? She dreaded him tiring of her, of his wearying of her peasant ways, of his hating the differences in their rank. 'But I would never leave him,' she whispered, half in protest.

And he will never leave you. He loves you.

She thought of the last time they had mated, tenderly, face to face. Earlier that day and for days before, she had been distressed and unsettled. She had hated the way that they no longer kissed when they joined.

Had he wanted me only for a child he would have had his way with me in the manner prescribed by the book. But Magnus loves me. He wanted to show me, to comfort and to treasure me. He wanted me to know it.

He had made love to her that night, face to face, body to body, kiss to kiss. The realization of what he had done, of why he had done so, of the sacrifice he had made, all dazzled her.

Magnus loves me enough to have done this for me, to make love to me in the most intimate, gentle way, although that very night had been our fifth time. Still he did so, because he wanted to reassure and comfort me.

Elfrida sat down with a thump and hugged her knees. Why had she not seen this earlier? Was it simply because of the missing girls and Silvester? Was it because of the petty malice of Lady Astrid, as Magnus thought? *No, I have been lacking in confidence, in my witch confidence, for several days.*

She touched her breasts and flinched, her nipples were so sore. She started to count days since her last monthly course. *I have not been myself. Could it be I am already with child? Is that what all this is?*

She laughed at the thought, at the wonder of it. *Do I tell Magnus? Do I let him try his 'magic' again on me?*

Do both! Still laughing, Elfrida scrambled to her feet and ran out of the solar-bedroom, rushing to find her husband, to tell him all their news. Darting into the yard, she spotted him a few moments later and her spirits soared when he saw her in turn and waved. As one they moved toward each other, Elfrida pounding over the cobbles of the manor yard, Magnus charging along the dusty track from the May pole and the church.

'Steady, lovely.' He caught her before she went sprawling across a cart rut in her haste to reach him and swept her over his shoulder.

'Hey!' Torn between laughter and indignation she snatched at his belt to steady herself. *Only Magnus would dare to haul me over his shoulder.* 'I have something to tell you, husband.'

'Good, for I have something to show you, wife.' Speaking, he transferred her more snugly into his arms and kissed her. 'Happy Midsummer, sweeting.'

He stopped in the middle of the track and kissed her still more deeply, ignoring the cat-calls of his men and the twittering swallows above them. 'Look,' he said, when they at last surfaced a little from their embrace.

Elfrida licked her lips to savor all of his kiss and tore her attention away from his loving eyes and mouth. Following his pointing finger she saw the old horse, Star, decked out in a shining new saddle and with ribbons plaited through his black mane. She was still smiling when Magnus lifted her onto the saddle and settled himself behind her.

'I thought since ladies like high horses we might ride one to our tryst. No, no.' He stopped her from riding astride. 'Ladies ride sidesaddle.'

'Witches do both,' she teased, relaxing into his arms again. 'A tryst?'

'Indeed, Elfrida, for I mean to court you as your gentle knight.' He clicked his tongue and Star plodded forward, tiny bells on his harness jingling sweetly. Star carried panniers, too, and Elfrida could see they were both full to bursting with wine, dates, cheese and all good things.

When has Magnus had time to prepare all this? He must have worked so hard and fast.

Delighted at the care of his courting, she felt easy enough with him to tease a little more. She raised her eyebrows. 'And when you flung me over your shoulder? Was that your courtesy in action?'

'That's the Viking in me.' He grinned and tightened his arms about her. 'Should I pay you a forfeit?'

'Only if you want to.'

*　*　*

She dimpled a merry smile at him, her amber eyes bright and limpid. He had not seen her so happy for days, and it made him realize how much he had missed her teasing. *Splendor in Christendom, I am so glad to see her more like herself.* It made what he must say next far easier.

'Elfrida, if I have been lacking in any way of late and rough in my manners, then I am sorry, truly sorry.'

He saw surprise break in her face and almost stopped but that would be cowardly. He must say all of it. 'I love you so much.'

'And I you.'

They rode on in perfect silence, past the church and the glittering May pole and the wildly dancing crowds, past

Peter whirling and twirling with Bertha and Susannah. Nudging Star with his heel he guided the placid bay horse toward the river and the woods.

Once they were hidden from the others by the trees he took a steadying breath and said more. 'I love you, Elfrida, and I want you to be content with me. When I saw your Christina this spring, saw how thrilled she was to be with child, I understood what joy children are to wives and women. Yet I am wounded, God alone knows how deeply. I feared — I feared I might fail you, be unable to give you a baby.'

She touched his scarred face, cupping his bristly chin in her small hand. Her comfort spurred him to admit the rest.

'And then you might decide to leave me. No one would think you wrong! So I — '

She pressed her fingers to his lips, her eyes as deep and clear as the summer twilight. 'Did you also think that as a witch I might cast a charm so I would not become pregnant?'

'No!' He spoke so loudly that Star shied and the bells in his mane clashed. 'No,' he said again, 'Not really. I mean, why should you? We love each other. We are man and wife.'

★   ★   ★

Elfrida heard the halting shame in his voice and felt the heat of shame in his strong scarred body. Even as she marveled at his confession, he stiffened and braced himself, sitting straight in the saddle, as if convinced she would curse him, or worse. *Poor Magnus. He does not know that his 'Not really' and the rest of his brave speech is a love-gift to me more real than any courtly wiles.*

'I would think no less of you if you had thought thus,' she said softly. 'It would be understandable that you might suspect it, given my skills. Yet you did not blame or accuse me of such, did you?'

'Damnation, woman, I would never

do that,' he growled, his grip tightening round her again.

'I know.' She was proud of his loving silence, even proud of his doubts. *My husband is no fool.* And instead of accusing her, Magnus, warrior to the last, had sought to solve the problem himself, by means of his book. *Which he does not need to tell me of, not yet.* She had a flash of foresight, of the two of them back at the manor house and snug within the solar, lolling on the bed and studying the book between them.

A very pleasant dream-to-be but now surely it was her turn to share. 'Can we walk a little?' Star was a lovely old thing but she wanted to tell her news with the good earth beneath them, not on the back of a horse.

Silently, Magnus drew rein, tethered Star to a hawthorn and lifted her down. 'Which direction?' he asked, with her still in his arms.

'Right here.' She tapped the oak tree behind him and he swung her lightly onto her feet. At once Elfrida began to walk, following a deer trail. She heard Magnus closing in and spoke to him.

'I have not been myself of late, too anxious even for me.'

She thought she heard a snort behind her but wisely Magnus said nothing.

'I thought it was because of the Lady Astrid and Tancred and the mirror they held up to me.'

'A false one. You are my wife.'

'Your wife and your witch.' It felt good to say both. 'Then, with all this recent talk of lost children and our search for missing children, I did not understand myself. But I do now.'

She stopped and turned to him. She took him in her arms, hearing the steady drum of his heart as she leaned against him. 'We are, that is, I am, no, we are — '

She broke off, wanting to say this well, wanting to see his face. She looked up at him. The love in his eyes made it simple to say. 'I am having your baby, Magnus.'

Glory shimmered in his face then,

making him whole again and beautiful. With warm, steady fingers he touched her cheek and forehead, brushed her shoulder, gathered her hand in his. 'When?' he murmured.

'Sometime after Christmas-time, possibly in Lent.'

'When the early lambs come. A lamb of our own.'

She smiled at the wonder in his voice and placed his palm on her belly. He cradled the tiny life there, accepting the babe. 'Ours,' she agreed.

'Ours.' He knelt amidst the bluebells and wrapped his arms about her, kissing her navel, resting his head against her as if searching already for another heart-beat within her. She ran her fingers through his black, straggling curls, traced a scar down his cheek to his patchy beard and chin.

'Clever lass,' he murmured. She felt a tear, his tear, soak into her blue silk sash. 'My clever lass.'

'Kiss me,' she whispered. 'Kiss me, Magnus. Make love to me as you have before.' She knelt within the shield of his arms and began to unpin the silk.

He gently plucked the pin from her and caught hold of her fingers. 'You are well, Elfrida? You will take no hurt?'

'Not a bit,' she said cheerfully. 'Neither myself nor the babe.' She unpinned the second brooch and the silk slithered from her shoulders, leaving her naked to the waist.

Now he reached for her, her Magnus, her husband and soon to be her lover. *Again*.

Elfrida smiled and let herself be overwhelmed, aware that their night together had only just begun — a summer bewitchment for them both.